KU-140-223

McFLANNEL
FAMILY AFFAIRS

HELEN W. PRYDE

THOMAS NELSON AND SONS LTD
LONDON EDINBURGH PARIS MELBOURNE
TORONTO AND NEW YORK

THOMAS NELSON AND SONS LTD
Parkside Works Edinburgh 9
3 Henrietta Street London WC2
312 Flinders Street Melbourne C1
5 Parker's Buildings Burg Street Cape Town

THOMAS NELSON AND SONS (CANADA) LTD
91–93 Wellington Street West   Toronto 1

THOMAS NELSON AND SONS
385 Madison Avenue New York 17

SOCIÉTÉ FRANÇAISE D'EDITIONS NELSON
25 rue Henri Barbusse Paris V⁰

———

First published 1950

McFLANNEL
FAMILY AFFAIRS

CONTENTS

DEDICATED TO
HOWARD M LOCKHART
AND THE SCORES OF MEN AND WOMEN
WHOSE VOICES AND ARTISTRY
HAVE GIVEN LIFE TO THE McFLANNEL CHARACTERS
IN THE BROADCAST SERIES

CHAPTER I

THE FAMILY TREE

I

WILLIE McFLANNEL was on his way home from work one evening when he was joined on the bus by an old acquaintance. Surprised and pleased, Willie exclaimed :

'It's yersel', McWincey ! Ah havenae seen ye since the Home Guard days ! Hoo are ye daein' ? '

Mr McWincey admitted that he was doing fine, and when the tussle to pay each other's bus fares had been settled by the conductor's choosing the more convenient coin, Willie asked if his friend was also on his way home from work.

'No,' was the reply ; 'as a matter of fact I'm on my way *to* my work.'

Willie took another speculative look at Mr McWincey's clothes, and asked if he was a baker, since he had such extraordinary hours of business.

'I'm not a baker,' retorted McWincey. 'As a matter of fact I've got no set hours—I just work till the job's done. Some days I'm through by four, but other times it takes me till midnight.'

'Jeengs, that's some job ! Are ye traivellin' fur dabbities or whit ? '

'As a matter of fact'—even the obtuse Willie noticed the overworked gambit this time—'although I do a lot of travelling I'm not trying to sell anything. It's like this—have you ever heard of folk wanting to find out about their ancestors ? '

'Huh—Ah would be feart to try an' fin' oot aboot mine.'

'So should most folk, if it comes to that, but as a matter

of fact heaps of people want to know if they're descended from this person or that. And that's my job—tracing ancestries.'

'D'ye tell me that? An' hoo d'ye go aboot it?'

Like the rest of folk, Mr McWincey was delighted to talk about his work. 'Oh, well,' said he, 'there's different ways. Sometimes I've got to spend hours in old churches looking up records. Sometimes I've got to go to Register House in Edinburgh. And now and again I get a trip up to London.'

'Guid fur you! An' are the folk aye wantin' a third leg tae kick theirsels wi' when ye fin' oot the truth?'

'Not at all. As a matter of fact, sometimes I find that quite poor people are descended from the real old aristocracy. There was an old woman once who——'

But Willie had no interest in old women. He interrupted with: 'D'ye get a bigger fee if ye've got guid news fur yer customers?'

'Oh,' was the complacent reply, 'I'm doing not too badly.'

Willie stroked his chin. 'Ye know, if Ah wisnae sae feart whit ye'd fin' oot, Ah'd ask ye tae hae a bit look intae the McFlannel forebears.'

'As a matter of fact, I was just this minute wondering if perhaps you're connected with the McWhannels—you know, a corruption of the name.'

'McFlannel—a corruption o' McWhannel?'

'If that's the case, you know, you'll be a sept of the clan McDonald and entitled to wear the McDonald tartan.'

The man's eagerness was almost his undoing; his would-be customer shrank away. 'Ach, the Black Watch tartan's guid anuff fur me. Ah wore it when Ah wis in the Glasgow Highlanders in the last war.'

'Yes, but it means so much more to have a family tartan of your very own!'

'Ach, Ah'm ower auld tae be wearin' the kilt nooadays.'

'Oh, but it's not just for the sake of wearing the kilt! There's the family pride and all that. Pride in knowing that you're descended from generations of fighting men.'

'Och, it's fightin' weemin we keep in oor faimly.'

'Does it not fire your blood,' went on the sales talk, 'to think that perhaps your great-great-grandfather had his own piper playing for him while he ate his dinner in a flagged dining-hall with the rafters blackened by age ?'

'Ay, an' peat reek—because the lum hadnae been swep'—if there *wis* a lum.'

The irreverent retort pained the far-from-matter-of-fact Mr McWincey. 'I don't think you're taking this very seriously, Mr McFlannel ! As a matter of fact, what put the name McWhannel into my mind was because I noticed in this morning's paper that there were some heirs missing in a McWhannel executry, and you might be the very man they're looking for, if—as I imagine is likely—McFlannel is a corrupt form of McWhannel.'

'Ay ? Ach—Ah'm no' botherin'.'

'But there's your family to think of, man ! For all I know, there's maybe some old mansion house waiting for somebody like Mrs McFlannel to take charge of it.'

'Ach, the wife's no' interested in mansion hooses,' replied Willie, speaking for himself.

'I never met the woman yet who wasn't interested in a bigger house. I think it's worth looking into, you know.'

Willie chuckled. 'Ah'm jist thinkin' oor Maisie wid be fair divertit tae be livin' in a hoose like that. Ma dochter, ye ken. She's a teacher—an' bung-fu' o' big ideas.'

'Have you any grandchildren ?'

'Ay—Ah've anither dochter mairrit—wi' twa weans. Ach, but they live in Edinburgh an' think they're the cat's pyjamas a'readies. It wid take a gey big mansion tae please theym.'

'Any sons ?'

'Ay—twa.'

'Well, what about their inheritance ? You owe it to them —it's your moral responsibility.'

'Here—that's anuff o' yer sales talk. Ah'm no' havin' ony.'

'It's *not* sales talk. I tell you what—if you'll just say the word, I'll look into this McWhannel business. If you've no connection with them, we'll say no more about it, but if you have and there's

3

something in this executry for you, we can arrange the thing on a commission basis. How's that?'

Willie pondered the point but turned it down with : ' Ach, Ah wid be like a coo wi' a gun in yin o' thae big hooses. Naw. Ah wid raither jist be the wey Ah am. A bonnie-like ticket Ah wid look takin' ma dinner in a hall wi' black rafters an' flags ower ma heid.'

' The flags would be on the floor, man ! '

' Away wi' ye ! It wid be sacrilege tae tramp on the Union Jack ! '

' I didn't mean that sort of flags—I meant the stone kind ! '

' Eh ? A stane flair ? Ah doubt the wife wid have somethin' tae say tae that. She's complainin' aboot 'er knees as it is.'

' What on earth have her knees got to do with it ? ' demanded McWincey.

' She wid have tae wash the stane flair ! '

' Not a bit of it, man ! She'd have servants to do that for her ! '

Willie tightened the knot of his tie, saying with determination, ' That feenishes it. Ah could swallow the piper, but no' servants staunin' watchin' me tryin' tae get peas ontae ma knife.'

' You know,' said the Ancestry Research worker, ' it's queer how one gets a wrong impression of people. I used to think, in the Home Guard, that you were a broad-minded chap—you always seemed quite keen to take up new ideas—not like some of the sergeants who were for ever cracking up what they did in the trenches in 1916. I'd be sorry to think you'd lost that resiliency of spirit.'

' Ach, them big words is ower much fur me. It's oor Maisie ye want tae talk tae. Ah tell ye whit—you have a deck at that McWhannel business an' come alang tae oor hoose some night an' tell us aboot it. Hoo long wid it take ye ? '

' Oh, give me a fortnight,' said McWincey, restraining a smile of triumph ; ' but I'll need to have some particulars about your-self first. Where you were born, what your father's name was and where he was born, all you can remember about your aunts and uncles.'

4

Having imparted the meagre statistical information at the disposal of his recollection, Willie left the bus and forgot all about the incident.

2

One evening, a fortnight later, he pushed away his empty pudding plate, wiped his mouth with the back of his hand, and said, 'Well, that's that ! We'll hae wur dinner noo.'

His wife was appropriately insulted. 'Willie !' she complained, 'it's right mean of you to say that—after you getting soup and meat and vegetables and a pudding !'

'Ach ay, but it's no' a decent meal till we've had wur cup o' tea.' Turning to his daughter he asked, 'An' whit've you been daein' wi' yersel' the day, Maisie ?'

'Oh, the usual things,' was the off-hand reply. 'Doing clerical work for the Education Authority.'

Her mother was shocked into saying, 'Oh, Maisie, surely teachers don't have to do clerical work !'

'Have we not,' retorted the girl. 'I spent hours today doing nothing else. I'd to make out statistics from the Class Register ; I'd the Savings Bank ; I'd the Meal Tickets to clear up ; I'd to make out a report about backward children *and* measure some others for clothing coupons.'

Her brother nipped in with, 'Never mind—as long as they pay you for being a teacher, you've no need to grumble. And look at the holidays you get !'

'Oh, there you go again !' snapped Maisie. 'Always rubbing it in about the holidays. If *you* had to work with a gang of wee hooligans like I've got——'

Peter was at the stage of political enthusiasms of one colour or another. 'In a properly organised state of society, where the value of every individual's work——' he began.

His father, assessing the passing zeal at its true value, shouted him down with, 'Ach, get'm a soap box, somebody !' but his mother fancied there was an intensity of colour about his statements that horrified her, and she laid hold of the lad's wrist, saying :

'Peter—that's an awful way to talk! I hope you're not turning into—into—' but the word with Iron Curtain associations was too much for her to utter. 'I mean——' she tried again.

'Don't worry, Mother,' put in Maisie, 'he's been reading *The Daily Bugle*. I saw that article myself. What the poor boob doesn't seem to realise is that the writer was arguing from a wrong premise.'

'He was not!' stormed Peter. 'And don't call me a poor boob! I'm old enough to think for myself. I'm not going to subscribe to the theory that what was good enough for my grandfather is good enough for me.'

'Huh!' The sneer came, as might be expected, from his sister. 'You're quoting now from his third paragraph, are you not? If you call that "thinking for yourself," then I've got another name for it.'

'Listen you to me!' commanded Peter, 'I don't care how tough your wee hooligans are—the work isn't any more exhausting than the precision work I'm doing, and yet you get three months' holiday and I don't even get three weeks.'

'We do *not* get three months' holiday!'

Willie felt it was time he was entering the arena. 'Away wi' ye, Maisie! Jist you add up a' yer Saturday mornin's—fifty-two half days make twenty-six whole days.'

The interruption didn't appeal to the girl, who retorted that she didn't work fifty-two weeks in the year.

'You're telling me!' remarked Peter pointedly.

'Here—that's enough!' said Sarah. 'Be quiet, the lot of you, and take your tea.' She handed her husband a cup and saucer; he took it, looking inquiringly at the bare tablecloth.

'Nothing tae eat alang wi't?' he asked. 'Nae cake?'

'I'll cake you! The very idea—after all the dinner you had!'

'A biscuit, well!' suggested Willie.

But biscuits, it seemed, were also out of the question, and from then the discussion between brother and sister took the well-worn route of food shortage, bad administration, faulty statesmanship and so back to the starting-point of the 'properly organised state of society' upon which Peter seemed to have set his heart. Just when it appeared in danger of starting on a return journey, Sarah turned the discussion into the by-path of holidays. Maisie immediately said that she was intending going a walking-tour holiday and could she have the loan of Peter's rucksack? Without giving a direct assent, Peter asked how she intended dressing for the tour—was she to be tempting the ants with her short pants?

'Peter!' exclaimed his mother. 'Don't be vulgar!'

Maisie, whose susceptibilities to vulgarity did not appear to be so keen as her mother's, merely remarked that the other members of the party would be wearing kilted skirts.

'Ach,' gargled Willie, 'weemin in kilts! Away wi' ye— weemin's hips make a mess o' a kilt.'

When this remark had been classified by Sarah as in the same category as Peter's, Maisie went on casually:

'I'd go in a kilt myself, only I'm not sure what tartan I'm entitled to wear.'

'Hodden grey?' suggested Peter. 'That's McFlannel tartan!'

At which Willie slapped his mouth. 'Tartan?' he ejaculated for no reason apparent to his household. Then he went on: 'Help ma boab Ah forgot! There's a chap comin' up tae see me the night.'

With the normal reactions of a housewife, Sarah demanded to know why she had not been informed earlier of this impending visitor; and anyway who was he?

'It's a chap that used tae be in the Home Guard alang wi' me. He's lookin' up wur ancestry. Ah met 'im a fortnight ago.'

His wife and daughter registered frank bewilderment; his son, however, took a different line.

'Well, Dad, you don't lack for spunk, to let anybody look very closely into the McFlannels' past tense!'

'Don't you jump tae the wrong conclusion, like a cock at a grosset!' retorted Willie. 'Ye'll sing a different tune if ye

7

hear that ye'll maybe some day be sittin' doon tae yer dinner in a dinin' hall wi' flags an' peat reek in the rafters an' a piper marchin' up an' doon.'

This somewhat muddled statement deepened the mystification of his women-folk ; Maisie's worry was for the state of her father's mental health, while Sarah's concern was all for the health of his body.

' Ah'm fine ! ' declared the man, addressing himself to both lines of inquiry. ' Ah'm jist tryin' tae tell Peter that the McFlannels isnae maybe sich scruff as he's aye makin' them oot tae be.'

' Dad,' said Peter quietly, ' try to explain to us in words of one syllable.'

' There's nothin' tae explain ! Ah'm jist waitin' fur this chap tae come an' tell me if Ah'm the long-lost heir that the McWhannels have been lookin' fur—an' if Ah am, ye'll can get wearin' the McDonald tartan in yer kilt, Maisie.'

The situation was fantastic, but due to her close attention to the romantic stories in her favourite weekly magazine, his wife was able to grasp things more quickly than might have been thought possible.

' Willie,' she blurted out, ' do you mean that—that you're maybe Sir somebody . . . ? '

' Ye never know,' replied Willie who, having embarked on this voyage of family vindication, must needs sail home.

' You're pulling our legs, Dad ! ' said Maisie.

' Ah am nut ! Ah jist hope it's *no'* true—that's a'. As Ah said tae this chap McWincey—Ah couldnae get peas tae stey on ma knife if there wis a lota servants gapin' at me.'

'Thuth-then,' stammered Sarah, 'maybe I'm Lady McFlannel?'

' Naw, ye widnae be Lady McFlannel ! '

' But I'm your wife ! '

' It's me that kens that—tae ma cost.'

Forgetting her attitude of incredulity, Maisie demanded, ' Then why can she not be Lady McFlannel ? '

' Because maybe wur name isnae McFlannel ! It's maybe McWhannel an' they're lookin' fur an heir tae some big hoose.

But Ah'm feart ye'll no' like it, Serah,' he added, turning to his panting spouse, ' the stane flairs wid be bad fur yer knees.'

Taking refuge once again in unbelief, Maisie advised her father to ' come off it.' Peter's observation was to the effect that this announcement might have been saved up, with more chance of success, for the First of April. Sarah, however, was swallowing the bait.

' Willie, say that again about the mansion house. Has it really got a stone floor ? '

Before he could answer, Maisie jeered : ' He means a flagged floor, Mother.'

' That's right,' said Willie cheerfully, ' the floor's flagged an' the rafters are black wi' age.'

' Sounds like circumstantial evidence, Maisie,' said Peter, then, dropping the banter, he went on : ' Dad, suppose you begin at the beginning and tell us the truth.'

But before Willie could do so, his wife's housewifely instincts prompted the complaint that he had no business inviting somebody to come to the house without first consulting her.

' McWincey's 'is name,' said Willie as though that explained everything.

' I would've put on the sitting-room fire if I'd known,' went on Sarah. ' Really, Willie, you're right aggravating, so you are.'

' Now, Mother, that's not the way to talk to Lord Midden-heid ! ' said Maisie, a remark that drew forth such a snapping reproof from her father that Peter observed jokingly that he must be in earnest.

' Of course Ah'm in earnest ! ' declared Willie.

' About this mansion house and us maybe being the heirs ? '

' No *us—me* ! '

' Where is it ? '

' Hoo should Ah know ? He never said.'

Maisie asked if it contained indoor sanitation and everyone listened for Sarah's time-worn reminder not to be vulgar. Instead, however, she flopped into a chair saying that her head was in a whirl and why was it that her husband had never told her about this possibility before and would he have to leave his work ?

'A bonnie-like ticket Ah'd look tryin' tae be a gaffer in a shipyaird dressed in a kilt ! ' was all the satisfaction she got.

Maisie gaped. 'Dad, tell us the truth. Is this, or is it not, a pipe dream ? '

'Ay—a bagpipe dream ! ' hooted Peter.

'Ye can mak' a fool o' me if ye like,' said Willie calmly, 'but Ah'm tellin' ye as sure as Ah'm sittin' here—that's whit McWincey said.'

In answer to her mother's grumble that it was awful careless of her father not to ask where the place was, Maisie suggested it would be at the back of beyond somewhere, and Peter's hoot rang out again as he added :

'We'll not need to use Youth Hostels now, Maisie ! We'll be able to walk from the south lodge to the shooting lodge every week-end.'

'My-my ! ' exclaimed Sarah. 'I wonder what Mrs M'Cotton'll say when she hears this ! She'll be fair chawed, so she will ! '

Which in turn drew from her husband the warning that she was not to ' blab ' until confirmation had been received, but the stricture hardly scraped the surface of her consciousness for she went on to say that she would need to get some new clothes ' for the sake of the new neighbours.'

'Haud yer horses, wumman ! ' bawled the parent-heir. 'We're no' there yet.'

'Oh—so there *is* some jookery-packery ! '

'There's no' ! ' Drawing a card from his pocket, Willie held it in front of his wife's eyes and read aloud : ' Andrew McWincey, Ancestry Investigator, 659 Bath Street, Glasgow. Inquiries treated in Confidence. Satisfaction Guaranteed.'

The sight of it was enough for Sarah. She was elated and said so in her own way.

'Good for you, Mother ! ' exclaimed Peter. 'Seeing anything in print's good enough for you,' but there was an affectionate note in his banter.

' Really,' continued Sarah, ' I don't know whether I'm on my head or my feet. This is just terrible. I don't know whether or not I'd like to be a Lady Somebody. Would *I* have to wear a kilt as well, Willie ? '

' Serah, if Ah ever see you wearin' a kilt, an' you wi' a beam-end like whit you've got, Ah'll—Ah'll '—he searched his mind for a suitably rash equivalent—' Ah'll buy a motor-bike ! '

' What for ? '

' Tae get away f'ae the sight o' ye ! '

3

From there the conversation drifted to a discussion of clan tartans, and their preferences had reached the pitch of an argument when the door-bell rang announcing the arrival of Mr McWincey. Sarah responded to the ring of fate with customary misgivings :

' Oh dear-dear, I wish I'd put the sitting-room fire on. Dear only knows what the man'll think—coming to tell us about being titled people and us sitting in the kitchen ! My heart's near choking me with excitement. What'll Mrs M'Cotton say to this ! '

When the introductions were over, Willie came straight to the point, by asking if there had been much difficulty finding out about the McFlannel family tree.

' No difficulty at all ! ' was the reply. ' Your forebears were all such celebrated people that it was one of the easiest jobs I've ever had.'

They crowded round him as he spread some papers on the table, Sarah declaring that this was just like something you read about in books.

' Are we descended f'ae the McWhannels ? ' demanded Willie.

' Not a bit of it. As a matter of fact you can trace your McFlannel ancestry right back to the beginning of last century ! '

' Oh, Willie, this is wonderful ! ' exclaimed Sarah all over again. ' Just wait till I tell—— '

' Here we are ! ' interjected Mr McWincey unsympathetically.

' Here's the first record. The name is spelt McFlannen, but that's neither here nor there.'

They looked over his shoulder as he pointed out the various items. Mother and daughter held hands breathlessly.

' In the year 1823 a William McFlannen was hanged for sheep-stealing.'

Willie snorted self-consciously ; the reactions of the others were less obvious.

' In 1846,' went on Mr McWincey, ' there was a Matthew McFlannen sent to prison for embezzling five hundred pounds.'

' Imagine that ! ' murmured Peter.

' In 1869 one Peter McFlannen married the daughter of his employer James M'Cotton.'

' Did you say " M'Cotton " ? ' asked Sarah, unwilling to believe.

' Yes, M'Cotton, who disowned the marriage and the young couple emigrated to Australia.'

' Oh dear-dear, this is terrible ! '

Said Maisie, ' That's one thing we'll have to keep dark from Mrs M'Cotton anyway ! '

' In 1892,' continued the investigator remorselessly, ' one Mary McFlannel, who was carrying on business as a rag merchant, was——'

' Oh stop—stop ! ' commanded Sarah. ' That's enough ! I don't want to hear any more. I'm black affronted.'

The man straightened his back along with the others as Peter made the categorical statement that if that was the McFlannel family tree he preferred a monkey puzzle. Quite suddenly there was the sound of a giggle ; incredibly it came from Sarah.

' Oh, what a relief ! ' she said. ' I'll not have to wear a kilt after all ! '

CHAPTER 2

MATTHA BROUGHT TO BOOK

I

SARAH was glad, when the excitement had died down, that she had had no chance to see Mrs M'Cotton and hint her hopes ; it took quite a week, however, for her to forget the might-have-beens. The incident had not even made any lasting impression on the younger McFlannels, who had had more than a hint, so that to Maisie there seemed nothing out of place about still pedalling the sewing-machine, one evening, in an honest attempt to save a few of her father's clothing coupons. The pedalling irritated her father.

'Heh, fur the luva mike, Maisie, can ye no' pipe doon wi' that shooin' machine ? Efter bein' in a shipyaird a' day Ah like a bit peace an' quiet when Ah come hame at night.'

'I'm nearly done, Dad,' said Maisie soothingly, ' but considering it's one of your garments I'm working on, you should pipe down yourself.'

'Whit garment are ye talkin' aboot ? '

'I suppose you would call it a sark if you got the chance. I've been turning the cuffs for you.'

The man changed the subject before the girl could point any further morals. ' When'll yer mother be back ? ' he queried.

'Oh, any minute now. Peter, if you want to know, is at a class.'

Paying no attention to the implied taunt, the man grunted, ' Ay, " Public Speakin' an' Debate." Huh, a chap like oor Peter that's gotten sichna gift o' the gab doesnae need tae improve on nature.'

Maisie-the-teacher, leaving off her sewing, turned to examine her homework as she replied, ' Oh, but, Dad, if this class helps him to get rid of his awful Glasgow drawl, then you shouldn't discourage him. Although I admit that's a point of view I could hardly expect you to appreciate.'

' Is that you haein' a bit dig at the wey Ah speak ? '

' Well, if the shoe fits——'

' Help ma boab ! ' The man in exasperation uncrossed and recrosssed his legs. ' Am Ah never tae hear the en' o' this ! ' But his fury did not stop his ears from hearing the sound of his wife's coming into the house. ' Here,' he barked, turning his vexation into another channel, ' whaur've *you* been a' this while ? '

Sarah looked the picture of injured innocence as she retorted, ' My goodness, what a way to speak to me ! You'd think I was a servant lassie that had to be in at a certain time at night.'

' Well '—the man searched his mind for an excuse for his manner which would preserve his own dignity and at the same time placate his wife—' Ah wis gettin' worried aboot ye ! A fine sonsy wumman like you could easy get clouted ower the heid fur the sake o' yer fat—seein' fat's so scarce.'

But his diplomacy had its shortcomings. ' Oh, Willie,' said Sarah in a hurt tone, ' what a thing to say, and you know how I feel about being fat.'

' Never heed him, Mother. He's got a perverted sense of humour. Did you enjoy the Guild ? '

Maisie's red herring was successful, for in a moment or two Sarah had sniffed away her oncoming tears and was telling them all about the new minister who was coming to the church, and what the Woman's Guild were going to give him as a presentation. The topic lasted until the door-bell rang. Going to open the door, Sarah found an old friend, Mrs McLeather, standing there, her face twisted in agitation.

' Mrs McLeather,' gasped Sarah, ' what's wrong ? '

In a dwam of misery the visitor accepted the unspoken invitation and entered the house, making her way almost blindly to the kitchen, where Willie, out of perversity, was at that moment undoing his collar and tie by way of a hint that the hour was late. Ignoring the gesture, Mrs McLeather approached him.

' Mr McFlannel—it's your brother.'

Bewildered, Willie paused in his efforts. ' Whit's he been up tae noo ? ' he demanded.

' Wait till I tell you. This forenoon I was washing out the close. It really wasn't my turn, but the milk boy had broken a bottle just outside my door. It wasn't *my* milk boy, you understand,' she went on in pains-taking and -giving detail, ' it was the woman's next door, but I knew I'd wait till Kingdom Come before *she* would do anything about it. Remember I told you about her, Mrs McFlannel ? ' She turned to Sarah for confirmation.

' Ay, but whit's a' this got tae dae wi' oor Mattha ? ' put in Willie.

' Wait till I tell you. I was busy making whorly lines round the edge of the close when a man comes into the close hirpling like a chair that's lost its hind legs, and says to me, says he, ' Can ye tell me where Mrs McLeather lives ? '

Sarah persuaded her guest to sit down, taking advantage of the gap in the monologue to say, ' The cheek of him ! '

' Oh, but that wasn't the best of it ! ' continued Mrs McLeather, ' wait till I tell you. I thought there was something familiar about him, then I minded seeing him at your flitting about fifteen years ago—or would it be nearer twenty ? '

' Never mind,' said Willie, who had no love for circumlocution, ' Ah'm waitin' tae hear the rest o' yer story.'

' Ay, but wait till I tell you,' repeated the woman insistently. ' When it dawned on me it was your brother Mattha I picked up my pail although I wasn't finished, and asked him just to come into the house.'

' And he slithered all over the whorly lines ! ' suggested Maisie in quiet amusement.

' How did you know ? ' exclaimed Mrs McLeather. ' That's just what he did. I could've warmed his ears, but he said he had **sore** feet and couldn't lift them.'

Restraining his natural instincts, Willie snapped, 'Ay, but whit happened efter that?'

'Well, the kettle was steaming away on the hob, so I thought I'd better offer him a cup of tea, seeing he was your brother, like, and while I was making it he began to tell me what a nice house I kept and all that. Real nice he was.'

'Oh dear-dear,' Sarah was preparing to wring her hands, 'you should've known he was after something when he carried on like that. But go on.'

'Well, I liked him fine to begin with. My own man's not awful keen to pass on any compliments. Well, we chatted away about you-folks for a while, and then, when we were finishing our tea, he asked me if I was needing any watches or clocks sorted.'

A murmur came from the vicinity of the sewing-machine to the effect that the Ethiopian was unable to change his skin, but the allusion was beyond the others.

'Shut up, Maisie!' barked Willie. 'Whit did ye say tae him when he asked ye that, Mrs McLeather?'

'I was just going away to say I had no clocks needing mending when he looked up at the mantelpiece and says he, "Here," says he, "there's somethin' gey faur wrang wi' that yin! It's pintin' tae five tae three an' it's only hauf past ten." So, just to put him off I told him I liked it that way. It strikes the hour at the twenty past, you see, and if you can't sleep at nights, it's cheery to lie and count up what time it is.'

The argument failed to convince anyone and Willie impatiently demanded that she should proceed with the narrative.

'Wait till I tell you! Before I could say knife he was up on his feet, grabbing my clock down off the mantelpiece and planking it on the table.'

'Dear Uncle-brass-neck-Matthew,' observed Maisie.

'Well, d'you know, if he hadn't been a brother of yours, Mr McFlannel, I'd 've told him where he got off, but seeing Mrs McFlannel and me's such old friends, like, I didn't want to hurt your feelings.'

Sarah's assurance that no-one had any tender feelings where

Mattha was concerned was interrupted by her husband's query,
'Did he waste yer clock, missus?'

'Wait till I tell you! It's one of those old-fashioned clocks
with a back door into the works and a front door for the pen-
dulum. So when he planked it down on the table he keeked
inside the back door and started blowing and spitting at the
dust—all over my table, butter and all—and then declared it
was needing a new hairspring or something.'

Willie's impatience turned to fury. 'Jeengs, he's an auld
twister. Ah'll wring 'is neck fur'm!'

'Oh, but that wasn't the best of it! Wait till I tell you!
I told him to put it back where he got it, but he said it was a
valuable antique and it was a fair disgrace to see it going to
wrack and ruin, and he went on and on at such a rate that I
began to believe him.'

'Oh, Mrs McLeather, you didn't!' exclaimed Sarah.

'Oh, but I did. And before I could stop him he was out
of the house and away—clock and all!'

Once again Willie's emotions changed, this time to soothing
assurance. 'Aw, but he'll bring it back, missus. He'll jist've
been tryin' to make a shillin' or two on the job.'

'That's as may be. But that's not what's worrying me—it's
what was inside the clock! I was washing up the tea things
tonight—I was extra late, for my man didn't come home till
eight o'clock—well, as I was saying, I was washing up the tea-
things when it came over me all of a sudden—*I'd put my new
clothing coupon book inside the front door of the clock*—to be safe!'

'Good gracious, clothing coupons!' blurted out Sarah and
her daughter simultaneously. Willie's reaction was to make
the observation that Mrs McLeather would, of course, have
her name and address clearly written on the document in
question.

'That's what's worrying me, Mr McFlannel! I always meant
to write it in, but somehow I forgot. Oh, I just don't know
what to do.'

'Ach, don't worry, missus. Ye'll get yer clock back.'

'Willie,' Sarah almost screamed, 'how can you be so stupid!

17

You know the kind of man Mattha is—as sure as anything he'll sell those coupons.'

'The funny thing is,' went on Mrs McLeather ruefully, 'I had my niece up seeing me last week, and she was telling me how hard-up she is for coupons, and her getting married and all, and I was tempted to offer her my book—especially when she said she'd do anything to get coupons. I wish I had. Oh, Mrs McFlannel, isn't it *awful* ! '

'It is that, Mrs McLeather,' said Sarah sympathetically, 'I'm real sorry for you, so I am ! ' Turning on her husband she added, 'Willie, you'll just have to go and see that brother of yours this very minute ! '

'Whit ? At this time o' night—an' me wi' ma collar an' tie aff ! '

Maisie decided to take a hand. 'But, Dad, don't you see you'll *have* to do something. It was for your sake that Mrs McLeather was kind to the old twister.'

'Hear, mind whit you're sayin' aboot my flesh an' bluid ! ' blustered Willie, at the same time searching in the empty spaces of his mind for a means of retreat. 'Ach, Mrs McLeather, Ah don't see whit ye're in sichna state fur. Wait an' you'll see—Mattha'll be up first thing in the mornin' wi' yer coupons.'

'But,' suggested Sarah deliberately, 'what if he's sold the clock to somebody without seeing the coupons were there ? '

'Whitna daft idea ! As if oor Mattha wid sell the clock ! He'll get mair affa Mrs McLeather fur repairin' it every fortnight.'

'I know what he'll get off me—and it'll not be money ! ' was the threat that came from the injured party.

At that moment Peter, returning from his study of the art and craft of public speaking, opened the door and gaped at them. Maisie explained the situation briefly.

'Our precious Uncle Matt has gone and pinched Mrs McLeather's clothing coupons ! '

'He never stole them,' shouted Willie in a further attempt to avoid resuming his neckwear, 'he jist took away 'er clock tae sort it, an' the coupons wis inside it ! '

' Coupons—inside a clock ? ' repeated Peter. ' What a queer place to keep things in ! '

' Sure—that's why I kept my coupons there ! ' Mrs McLeather was determined to justify herself. ' I thought if the house was burgled any time nobody would ever think of looking there.'

' D'you know, Mrs McLeather,' said Maisie, ' I wouldn't put it past the old sinner to have had his eye on the coupon book all the time ! '

' No, Maisie, he couldn't've seen it from where he was sitting,' said Mrs McLeather in an access of fairness ; ' it's a glass door on the front of the clock, but it's the kind of glass you can't see through. And forbye he never had the door open at the front at all.'

To Peter's query as to why she hadn't gone to the culprit's house and made sure, Mrs McLeather retorted that she did not know where he lived.

' You go, Peter,' said Sarah ; but Maisie exclaimed, ' Just a minute, folks. We'll have to go about this very carefully. Supposing Uncle Matt *hasn't* seen the coupon book and you ask him if he has—don't you see he'll deny all knowledge of it and snaffle the book as soon as your back's turned ? '

' Oh dear-dear,' wailed Sarah, ' it's terrible to have a scoundrel in the family ! ' Which brought upon her the wrath of the scoundrel's brother. When peace had been restored Maisie suggested that Uncle Matt should be fetched to their presence under some pretext or other.

' I know,' said Peter, ' I'll go along to his house and tell him our kitchen clock has stopped and we want him to come and start it.'

' There's naething wrang wi' wur kitchen clock, but ! ' interposed the literal-minded Willie.

' All right, I'll soon make sure there is ! ' Peter took a step in the direction of the mantelpiece as he spoke. ' Since you've got such a passion for the truth, Dad——'

And before his father could interfere, Peter had laid the clock on its back. Willie was furious, declaring that the time-piece had not lost a minute in the last six weeks ; but before he could set it upright again Maisie had got in with, ' Do you want to see your brother in prison, Dad ? '

' Naw, but Ah'm no' wantin' oor Mattha tae lay hauns on it ! '

In answer to Peter's suggestion to leave the matter until the next day, Mrs McLeather burst into tears, saying, ' Oh, Peter, I don't think I'll can sleep till I know what's happened to my coupons ! '

' All right, I'll fetch him here inside half an hour,' said Peter.

' Naw ! ' the protest came from Willie who seemed in pain, ' Mattha's no' tae monkey wi' that clock ! '

' Okay, Dad,' answered Maisie soothingly, ' I'll promise you he won't touch it. Now listen : we don't want to confront the old rascal with Mrs McLeather right away—that would only put him on his guard. I tell you what, Peter, you bring him into the kitchen here, and Dad and Mother and Mrs McLeather will be in the sitting-room.'

' Whit,' Willie looked affectionately at his discarded collar and tie, ' on a cauld night like this ! '

' We can put on the electric fire,' said Sarah. ' What then, Maisie ? '

Maisie was enjoying herself. ' That means I'll be left alone with Uncle Matt and the kitchen clock.'

' Ah said *naw* ! ' bellowed her father.

When he had been pacified by the assurance that Maisie's intentions were to pretend to be in desperation for coupons wherewith to negotiate the purchase of a new coat, Peter went off on his errand, and the others, in varying moods of compliance, disposed themselves according to Maisie's instructions. Twenty minutes later Peter's voice was heard in the lobby assuring his uncle that his interview with Maisie would be *tête-à-tête*.

2

' Ach, this is a terrible-like cairry-on,' grumbled the visitor adenoidally. ' Draggin' me oot at this time o' night. Could ye no' 've brung the nock doon tae ma hoose ? ' Catching sight of Maisie's face he was unaffected by its comeliness, for he continued his complaints : ' Ah wis jist tellin' Peter comin' up the road there that Ah'm no' fit fur ja'nts at this time o' night.' Turning to his nephew for concurrence, he was surprised to see the young man disappear behind a closing door. ' Whit's up wi' him ? ' he demanded.

' Goodness knows,' said Maisie, indicating a chair.

Brushing aside the courtesy, Mattha demanded to know what was wrong with the clock that it was lying on its back.

' Just a minute, Uncle Matt,' whispered Maisie. ' While there's nobody else here—I wondered—could I—well, as a matter of fact there's a rather delicate matter I'd like to broach.'

Spelling never having been his strong point, Mattha exclaimed, ' A brooch ?   D'ye want me tae get a brooch fur ye wholesale ? '

Dousing the glim in his eyes, Maisie said she didn't mean that kind of brooch, and—could she speak to him confidentially ?

Mattha sat down in his eagerness to do business.

' You know—um—' Maisie felt she was putting up such a good performance that it was a pity it was being wasted on so small an audience. ' You know that when a girl's—well, hoping to get married, she—she likes to have a well-stocked bottom drawer ? '

' Ah get ye ! ' was the reply through lips that had to be moistened. ' Ye mean ye want me tae gie ye lines fur the wholesale ? '

' Well, lines aren't much use by themselves nowadays, if you know what I mean ! '

' Ay.   Ah ken fine.   It's clothin' coupons ye're efter.'

' Shsh !   Don't shout ! '

' Well, it jist so happens Ah can help ye oot—in the wey o' business, of course.   A hale new book—never been yased.'

' How much ? ' demanded Maisie.

He hedged. ' Well—ehm—depends hoo much ye're needin' them.'

' How much did *you* pay for them ? '

' Well, it wis like this, see.   An auld buddy says tae me,

" Here," says she, " here's a coupon book that's nae use tae me—Ah havenae got the money tae buy claes wi' ! " '

At that the door opened and Mrs McLeather practically jumped into the kitchen shouting, ' It's a dirty lie ! '

The surprise brought Mattha to his feet. ' Whit are *you* daein' here ? ' he barked.

' We've all been standing at the back of the door listening ! ' continued Mrs McLeather in the same volume of sound. ' You old rascal, give me back my coupon book ! '

Pointing an accusing finger at Peter, Mattha yelped, ' Ah've been framed, so Ah have. It's you that's the swindler fur bringin' me up here tellin' me lees aboot yer kitchen nock.'

' I didn't tell any lies,' said Peter, ' I only said the clock was stopped and would you come and look at it.'

Willie stepped forward. ' Come on, Mattha, haun' ower that coupon book ! '

' Ah don't ken onythin' aboot hur coupon book, but ! ' declared Mattha.

' You tried to sell it to Maisie the now ! ' shrieked Mrs McLeather.

' Ah could bash ye, so Ah could, Mattha,' said Willie, ' ye're a disgrace tae the faimly ! '

Mattha tried to escape. ' Let me oota here. The wife'll be worryin' aboot me.'

' She'll worry a lot mair afore Ah'm dune wi' ye. Come on, man. Haun the thing ower.'

' Ah'm tellin' ye,' roared Mattha to Sarah's consternation, for she was excessively neighbour-conscious, ' Ah havenae got it ! '

' I think you have,' said Maisie quietly ; ' in fact you were just reaching for it when the door opened just now.'

' Ye're a durty lota crooks, so ye are ! ' snarled Mattha, clapping his hand protectively over his breast pocket.

' How much did you get for Mrs McLeather's clock when you pawned it ? ' asked Peter.

Guilt was written all over Mattha's face as he gulped, ' Wha tellt ye ? Ah mean——'

Mrs McLeather moaned, ' Oh—pawned ! This is awful. My poor old clock in a pawnshop—where it's never been in its life ! '

The cumulative effect of accusation caused Mattha to blurt out that he would get the wife to them, so he would. As for Mrs McLeather she grasped Willie's arm and pleaded with him to use his influence to get her clock out of its degrading surroundings. Maisie said she thought they should all sit down calmly and discuss the matter.

' Calmly ? ' Mrs McLether was on the verge of a hysterical outburst. ' I like that ! And him stealing my coupons ! '

' Ah never stole them ! ' insisted the accused.

' You did so—they were in the clock ! '

Mattha's ' Eh ? ' might have been an expression of genuine surprise but his brother chose to interpret it as play-acting.

' See here, you ! ' he stormed, ' there's nae use you tryin' tae kid us on ye don't ken onythin' aboot the coupons. Staun' up straight, man, an' tell us first hoo much ye got on the clock.'

' A coupla quid,' he admitted after a slight pause for calculation, then, after a further calculation he added, ' Ah mean— three quid ! '

' Ah heard ye the first time ! ' rapped out Willie. ' Whit did ye dae wi' the money ? '

' Ah—Ah spent it—in the wey o' business ! '

' But my clothing coupons ! ' cried Mrs McLeather. ' What about them ? '

' Ah never touched them.'

' Come-come, Uncle Matt,' put in Maisie, ' don't say you're a liar as well as a thief ! '

' Oh, whitna language tae use—an' you a teacher ! ' Expecting to be backed up by the girl's refined mother, he was disappointed when no comment was forthcoming, so he went on, ' Ah'll get the polis tae ye ! '

' Peter,' continued Maisie, ' have a look in the inside pocket of his jacket.'

Seeing his nephew descending upon him, Mattha once again clapped a protective hand over his breast. ' Naw, it's no' ! Wullie, make 'im let me go ! ' Then, catching a look of evil intent in his brother's eye, he almost fell on his knees in his eagerness to protect his feet. ' Aw, Wullie, don't tramp on ma corns ! '

' Fork oot that coupon book, well ! ' said Willie, staying his purposes.

' Ah cannae—oh naw, ye'll murder me if ye touch ma sair corns ! '

' See's the book, well ! '

' But Ah'm tellin' ye Ah never . . .' began Mattha, but the foot of retribution fell and his sentence trailed off into a yelp of pain.

' Are ye wantin' some mair ? ' asked Willie, his foot poised for further punishment.

' But it's no . . .' Mattha started out once again, then, thinking better of it, he reached into his pocket and brought out the required article. ' Here ye are—but it's highway robbery, so it is ! '

Mrs McLeather seized the clothing coupon book, flicking over the pages in response to Maisie's suggestion that she should check up that it was intact.

' Ye've nae business sayin' sichna thing, Maisie ! ' complained her uncle ; then, nursing his feet ostentatiously, he bewailed his lot, ' Ah don't ken hoo Ah'm tae get hame the night.'

Willie halted his hirple towards the door. ' We've still tae settle the business aboot the clock ye pawned. Twa pound, ye said.'

' Three ! '

' Ye said twa the first time. Whit did ye dae wi' the money ? '

' Oh, Mr McFlannel,' pleaded Mrs McLeather, ' give him the money to get it out the pawn and I'll pay you back tomorrow ! '

' Wait yer hurry, missus ! ' replied Willie. ' He's got tae pey it up 'issel'. See's the pawn ticket, Mattha ! '

' Ah havenae got it wi' me,' said Mattha ; then, seeing the tentative move of his brother's foot in the direction of his corns, he dived once more into his pocket and brought out the document in question. Peter, peering over his father's shoulder, pointed out that there must be some mistake, for the amount indicated was fifteen shillings.

'That's right,' said Mattha, 'that wis a' they gien me—it wis sichnan auld nock ! '

Once again the company expressed themselves with some freedom of speech ; then Sarah, taking pity on her friend, shouted the others down with :

' Mattha McFlannel, if it wasn't that I don't want the family name dragged into the court, I'd send for the police right away. You're a downright rascal, so you are, and you'll come to a bad end. You get Mrs McLeather's clock out of the pawn first thing in the morning ! '

Under threat of further third-degree methods, Willie made Mattha promise to return the clock as suggested, and, eager to get home, Mattha made a crab-like exit without any pause for the minor courtesies. As soon as the door was closed Sarah went to the scullery to prepare the supper. At first Mrs McLeather was unwilling to wait and share the meal, but she was persuaded that after all the excitement she required a little relaxation. She sat down, saying, ' Well, I admit I *am* feeling a bit wabbit after all that carry-on. Here—I better put my coupon book away safe in my handbag. It's a bit the worse of the wear since I saw it last ! '

She held it out for inspection ; glancing at it Sarah exclaimed, ' Oh, it's filthy ! My—isn't that like Mattha ! He seems to make a mess of everything he touches ! See and put it into one of the inside pockets of your handbag so's to be sure it's safe ! '

' I will that ! ' declared Mrs McLeather ; then a moment later the family were horrified by a shriek : ' Here—look what's in the inside pocket of my handbag ! *My own coupon book.* It must've been there all the time ! '

' Jinglin' Geordie ! ' gasped Willie. ' So oor Mattha never pinched it efter a' ? '

They all stood round her in mute discomfort. ' Oh ! Do I feel ashamed of myself ! ' was all Mrs McLeather could say.

' But wait a minute ! ' Peter was the first in the audience to find his voice. ' Whose book *is* that dirty one ? '

' He must have pinched it from somebody else ! ' observed

Maisie, then, catching sight of her brother's twinkling eyes, she led a duet of laughter.

' Whit's bitin' you two ? ' demanded their father.

' Just think, Dad,' gurgled Peter, ' just think what a " had " Uncle Matt's going to get tomorrow morning when he planks down his fifteen bob on the pawnbroker's counter—and then finds there's no coupon book in Mrs McLeather's clock after all ! '

But there was more grimness in the man's face than amusement as he reflected on his brother's propensities. Perhaps he was visualising further chiropodist torture.

CHAPTER 3

BIDDY

IT was some weeks before Mattha ventured another call on his relations. Since their own conduct in the affair had not been noticeably dignified, they decided to let the matter drop. A certain amount of embarrassment robbed Sarah's welcome of its heartiness when she eventually opened the door to him one evening. He seemed, for his part, oddly reluctant to accept the invitation to enter, wanting to know first of all if there were any visitors in the house. Reassured, he made a furtive entry, and not even his brother's welcome appeared to put him at his ease.

'Ah cannae complain,' he said, when asked how he was keeping; then, although the offer of a chair was almost insistent, he declined to accept it until they had both reiterated the information that he was not 'in the road.'

'Whit's up wi' ye?' asked Willie bluntly.

'Ach, Ah'm fine.'

'You don't look very fine!' Even his sister-in-law, who never looked at him directly if she could avoid it, observed the change. 'It's at home you should be—in your bed!'

'Naw-naw. Ah'm maybe a wee-thing peched wi' sclimmin' yer stairs. Wi' us-yins bidin' in the close Ah'm no' yased wi' stairs.'

'An' hoo's business?' asked Willie, blundering upon what his wife felt was dangerous ground. 'Whit wis ye sellin' the day?'

'Ach—ehm—Ah cannae mind!'

Which was such an extraordinary statement that Sarah began to be afraid he was going to be ill on the spot; she therefore suggested with more urgency than tact that he ought to go home immediately.

'Naw. Naw. No' that! Naw.' There was genuine fear in his tones.

At that moment the door-bell rang and he jumped to his feet jittering, 'Wha's that?'

Sarah said she was sure she didn't know, while Willie told him to pull himself together, that if it was the police force, then he had had it coming to him for a long time. In a sudden access of courage Mattha stated categorically that he was not afraid of the police—this time. All the same, as soon as his brother had gone to open the outside door, Mattha made a tentative move in the direction of the scullery.

'What are you going in there for?' demanded Sarah.

'Och—ehm—nothin'. Ehm—Ah wis jist gonnae get a drink o' water.'

'Well, sit down and I'll get it for you!'

But before she could do so the visitor had disappeared among the culinary utensils, shutting the door after him. As soon, however, as it was discovered that Willie had admitted Maisie, Mattha ventured out once again into the blaze of the kitchen light. With a certain lack of compassion Sarah asked if he had found the tumbler in the dark.

'Oh—ehm, Ah wisnae thirsty efter a'.' He sat down, acknowledging his niece's greeting, stating that he was in perfect health. Pressed for details, he admitted that his corns were giving him no trouble.

'Don't tell me ye've fun' a cure fur them at last!' said Willie.

'Naw, naw. It's jist that—well, Ah jist forgot Ah had them, like.' He shifted uncomfortably in his chair, smoothed his cap over his knee, cleared his throat, and asked Maisie, 'Did ye see onybody?'

'Anybody?' repeated Maisie, partly in correction of his pronunciation and partly in interrogation. 'Where? When?'

There was no reply except the shake of a head.

'There's something wrong with him, Maisie,' said Sarah. 'I knew the minute I opened the door to him and he hadn't a parcel in his hand. He can't even remember if he sold anything today.'

Once more the door-bell pealed and once more Mattha jumped to his feet, gasping, ' Wha'll that be this time ? '

' I don't know,' said Sarah, going to the door, ' but if you're wanting another drink of water while I'm finding out, you'll get a tumbler on the shelf.'

But instead of making for the scullery, Mattha stared speculatively at the folding-down bed-settee as though wondering what its chances were in the way of a hiding-place, and by the time he had made up his mind the scullery was a safer bet, the need for it had passed, for the voice of Mrs M'Corduroy, the next-door neighbour, could be heard distinctly. That lady, true to her use and wont, had called to borrow something, so Mattha sat down once again on the edge of the chair.

' I wish you'd come clean,' said Maisie.

' Ach, Ah hadnae time tae wash masel' afore Ah came oot the noo.'

For the next few minutes Willie lectured his brother on the psychology of fear, although he would not have given such a grandiloquent name to the process which he himself described as ' bringin' Mattha's backbone tae the front.' A particularly lusty gale of laughter from the outer door put an end to the lecture, the audience having jumped to its feet in alarm.

' It's all right,' said Maisie, ' it's only Mrs M'Corduroy. She's got a voice like an old sheep with asthma.'

Instead of subsiding, however, Mattha asked if they had a bed in their ' room.'

' Yes, but Peter sleeps in it,' Maisie informed him.

' Ah'm no' wantin' it fur sleepin' in, but ! Is it yin o' thur new-fangled kind like this yin ? '

' Naw, it's a box-bed, but it widnae be nae guid tae ye eithers fur crawlin' ablow. Serah's got it bung fu' o' tin trunks an' hampers an' things.'

Sitting down to think up some new place of refuge from his unspecified fears, he kept silence until Sarah returned. Then he asked what kind of bed they had in Matt's room. Sarah, unaware of his predilection, snapped :

'It's a modern bed with an interior spring mattress, the very latest, so you needn't be trying to sell us anything like that!'

'Ah wisnae . . .' began Mattha, when Willie tried once again to soothe his troubled spirit.

'Come on ower tae the fire, man! Draw in yer chair. There's Maisie away tae pit on the kettle fur a wee cuppy tea.'

'It's no' tea Ah'm needin', but!'

Refusing to believe that he would expect anything more stimulating in such a totally abstinent house, Sarah pleaded with him to tell them what was worrying him.

'Nothin's worryin' me!' he declared; then, as the outer door banged and Peter's tuneless whistle was heard, he started to his feet all over again.

'It's Peter, ya dooly!' shouted Willie. 'Hame f'ae the night school.'

'The Technical College!' The correction came from the student's mother.

'Will there be onybody along wi' 'im?' Mattha looked utterly terrified.

Even when Peter came into the kitchen he was still concerned.

'Hoo' ye,' he greeted without waiting for a reply, 'did ye see onybody lookin' fur—Ah mean—ye're jist yersel'?'

'I am—but I don't think you are!'

Only partly satisfied, Mattha sat down again and allowed the conversation to flow past him. He had the look of a man listening to the erection of his own gallows. The banter to which Peter was being subjected had no interest for him—in any case most of it would have been unintelligible to him, consisting as it did of a jingle of psychological terms which Peter, under the auspices of the Workers' Educational Association, had been picking up. Pointing good-naturedly at her uncle, Maisie asked Peter if—speaking as an amateur psychiatrist—he would say the man was suffering from a fixation. Dimly aware that he was being spoken to, Mattha retorted:

'Ah am nut sufferin' f'ae asphyxiation—but Ah will be when the wife gets a haud o' me.'

' Your wife ! ' gasped Sarah. ' So that's it ! You're hiding from her ! '

Willie, speaking from a lifetime's experience of imaginary henpeckery, said, ' It's surely no' as bad as that ! '

To which his brother replied, ' Oh, is it no', is it no' ? ' Then, as the door-bell pealed vociferously, he dropped his defiant manner and yelped, ' There ! Whit did Ah tell ye ! Oh, don't let 'er in ! ' Laying a restraining hand on Sarah, he went on, ' Aw, Serah, don't go tae the door. She'll murder me, as sure's daith ! '

Flinging off his hand, Sarah obeyed her instincts of hospitality, leaving her husband to deal with the whimpering Mattha. She opened the door and her sister-in-law strode in without waiting for the formality of an invitation.

' Let me get me hands on him, the miserable son of a pig ! ' yelled Biddy in the byegoing. In the kitchen she paused, ' Ah, there ye are, ye blisterin' son of a thief ! Stand out from behind your brother and take what's comin' to ye ! '

Mattha cringed still further behind his brother. ' Aw, Wullie, she's gonnae bash me ! '

' Bash ye ! Oi wouldn't be soilin' me hands on such a trifle as bashin'. It's morderin' ye Oi'm afther.' Her sister-in-law tugging at her for an explanation of the circumstances, Biddy shrugged her off with, ' Did he not tell you ? He's taken me mother's picture—the little brooch Oi wore at me neck when Oi was all dressed for the Church—the little picture that's all Oi've got left of her—me dear dead mother that was mounted in gold—he's taken it and sold it ! '

The accuser having broken down sobbing, Sarah took up the cudgels.

' Oh, Mattha, you didn't ! '

' Now ye needn't be denyin' it ! ' shrieked Biddy when Mattha opened his mouth in self-defence. ' Oi've soffered all me married loife. You torn me house into a shop so that Oi can't ever be keepin' it toidy. You break me heart with your promises to mend your ways and you never doing it.'

' Aw, but Biddy——'

' And your corns and your corns and your corns. Oh, it's

me that's sick to death with your corns. And now this—me mother's own picture ! If she was standin' here she'd be tornin' in her grave ! Me that was always the favourite of all her childer —and it was fourteen she had and three of them twins ! ' She sobbed for a moment, then, courage returning, she reached out an arm screaming, ' Come out of there, you wretched little worm, and Oi'll draw the chicken heart out of you.'

' Shsh, Biddy ! ' said Sarah. ' Not so loud. The neighbours'll hear you.'

' And what for should Oi be carin' ? '

' Hiv ye no' a word tae say fur yersel, Mattha? ' demanded Willie.

' She'll no' gie me the chance ! '

' And what for should Oi be givin' you the chance ? Ye stole me mother's brooch, didn't ye, now ? '

' Ah never ! Ah jist took the len' o't ! '

' Give it me back again. Come on, give it me ! ' and she held out a rapacious hand, unclean as the claw of a vulture.

' Ah—Ah cannae ! ' stammered the guilty party.

' Whit did ye dae wi't ? ' The bark came from Willie.

Mattha unable to say any more than ' Ah—Ah . . .' Biddy renewed her tirade. ' There ye are ! Ye stole it ! Now don't be denyin' it ! Oh, me poor dead mother's face in the hands of a stranger that she'll never see ! Oh, why didn't Oi be heedin' her when she warned me against you, Mattha McFlannel.'

Stepping aside suddenly, Willie pushed his craven brother into the forefront of the battle. ' There—tell us whaur ye've planked the thing.'

' Ah—Ah gien it tae a man—in the wey o' business.'

' Why ? ' asked Sarah. ' Did he give you money for it ? '

' Ay, it wis like this, see . . . ' he began sullenly, then surprisingly brightened up as an idea seemed to strike him. ' It wis a' your fau't, Serah ! ' Paying no attention to the gasp this statement drew forth, he went on : ' Ye mind thon braw electric fire that ye widnae buy affa me ? '

' It wis second-hand an' fa'in' tae bits,' said Willie.

' With an obsolete cable ! ' put in Peter, while Maisie added her quota to the effect that it required a vase of flowers to hide the chips in the enamel.

'Well, if youse hadda bought it affa me,' continued Mattha when the identification parade appeared to be over, 'Ah widda hin the money tae pey cash fur the typewriter.'

'Typewriter?' queried Maisie. 'Don't tell us you intended writing to the papers!'

'Hah!' Peter hooted. 'Now we know who "Pro Bono Publico" is!'

Shouting down her husband's request not to be slandered, Biddy wanted to know what all this had to do with her brooch. 'Oi want me brooch back—this noight as iver was!'

'But Ah'm tellin' ye, Biddy—ye cannae get it back! The man Ah gien it tae is away tae Aiberdeen!' Then, as Mattha felt his wife's hot breath bearing down upon him, there was a general scuffle in which Willie complained that his hair parting was being spoiled. It was Peter who managed to haul the infuriated woman to the other side of the kitchen, trying to soothe her en route by telling her that a combination of forces would get her treasure restored to her.

'From Aberdeen? Never! Leave me go, Peter, till Oi tear him from limb to limb for doing this to me.'

'But it wisnae ma fau't!' yelped Mattha from the other corner. 'I tellt ye! It wis Serah's!'

Before Sarah could say a word in self-justification, Biddy suddenly changed her tactics. 'Well, then, if ye'll not let me morder him, ye can keep him. Oi'm going back to Oireland where Oi should never have left.'

'But we don't want him!' In her exasperation, Sarah's tones lost their customary gentility.

'Neither do Oi!' Biddy's tones in turn grew a shade coarser, which caused Sarah to hiss : 'Shsh!'

'Shsh yourself! If Oi go back to Oireland you'll have to look after him *and* his wretched ould uncle into the bargain.'

'I will not! Willie, can you not say something?'

'See here, Mattha——' began Willie, when Biddy cut in.

'And what would you be sayin' "See here Mattha" for?

It's me that's to be reckoned with. You fetch me me brooch back.'

Willie tried arbitration. 'Hoo much wid it cost tae buy a new yin ?'

'Oi don't want a new one. How could Oi be getting a new picture of me mother and her in her grave these thirty years and more ?'

'Well, then, Mattha, whit aboot you goin' tae Aiberdeen efter the man ?'

Mattha shook his head so despairingly that all Willie's reluctant suspicions came to life.

'Help ma boab, Mattha, Ah cannae fur the life o' me understaun' hoo onybody wid gie ye money fur the photy o' an auld Irishwumman.'

Now it was Willie's turn. Biddy almost spat at him. 'Hould your whaysht, man ! You're talkin' of me mother that would be aloive today if I hadn't married that son of a pig in the corner there. Come out, Mattha McFlannel, and get what's comin' to ye !'

'Haud yer horses, wumman !' Willie showed her a good example by holding her by both elbows. Over his shoulder he threw the question once again to Mattha : 'Hoo much did ye get for the photy ?'

'Ah never got nothin' fur the photo ! It wis the brooch the man wanted. He said the settin' wis antique !'

'Well, hoo much did ye get fur the settin' ?'

Mattha hummed and hawed and eventually admitted that he had got five pounds for the article. Seeing a calculating look in her husband's eye, Sarah almost shouted :

'Now Willie, don't you go putting your hand in your pocket ! Let Mattha and Biddy dree their own weird.'

Her hopes thus dashed, Biddy started to moan all over again, saying that she would catch the first boat in the morning and in the meantime she would go home and fetch the few belongings of Mattha and his adjectival uncle. All of which put Sarah in such a state of alarm and despondency that she was willing to negotiate with Mattha in an attempt to recover the lost property.

When she discovered, however, that Mattha would require twenty pounds before the transaction could be carried through with any reasonable amount of success, she was less eager. Despair haunted Biddy's voice as she declared :

' Oi suppose Oi'll just have to be getting back to me old home in Oireland. It's ashamed Oi'll be to look at me mother's grave in the face.'

' Well, you'd better take Mattha with you ! ' was Sarah's suggestion, which Mattha turned down emphatically, insisting that he was ' bidin' here.'

' You are not ! ' By way of adding exclamation marks to her speech, Sarah shook her brother-in-law : ' Really, Mattha, I don't know how you could be so heartless as to give away the only photo Biddy had of her mother ! '

' But Ah never gien it away ! ' Self-righteousness bristled from every one of Mattha's pores. ' The man said he couldnae stick the sight o' the ugly mug in the settin', so he took it oot. Ah've got it in ma pocket.'

Biddy fell on the scrap of paper which her husband scraped from among the debris in his pocket. ' Oh, Glory be, it's me poor dead mother's face.' And she burst into such heartrending sobs that even the younger generation deriding in the background were forced to turn away their embarrassed faces ; then, the sobs subsiding, their aunt crooned over the fragment of paper so that Sarah, oddly moved, went over to where she stood and said :

' I tell you what, Biddy. We'll all club together to buy you a new brooch for the photo. How would that do ? '

' It's real kind of you.' She dried her tears and exhibited the picture in the palm of her hand. ' Look, Sarah, was she not the fine-looking woman ! '

The good looks, thought Sarah, must be more obvious to Biddy than to other people ; nevertheless she did as was expected of her and admired the portrait while the others drifted off on ploys of their own. Tea was served in an atmosphere of amity such as had not existed between the in-laws for years. Indeed, so much at home did Biddy feel that the fountains of her native

35

eloquence poured forth until all present were drowned in the flood of reminiscences. Her husband, not feeling compelled to exhibit that intensity of interest which his relatives bestowed with such courtesy on the narrator, retired within himself. Since taking off his boots his physical comfort was assured and his mind was free to devote itself to other schemes ' in the way of business.'

' Heh, Serah,' he said at the first lull, ' Ah ken a man that could get ye a new settin' fur that photy cheap.'

CHAPTER 4

THINGS THAT GO BUMP IN THE NIGHT

I

POLLY McFLANNEL was now both chronologically and spiritually Mrs M'Cotton the Second. At the moment she was having some domestic trouble in her home in Edinburgh. Her younger child, Moira, was going through a series of mild infectious troubles, and when she contracted mumps it was decided to send her brother Ian to stay for a few days with his grandparents. The news was not received with any noticeable pleasure on the part of either the hosts or the guest, Sarah for her part doing her best to make up for the erratic discipline of the child's parents and Ian doing his best to see to it that she got a run for her money. On the second night of his stay, a message came that Sarah's friend Mrs McLeather was ill and wanted to see her, so, leaving Maisie in charge of the sleeping child, she went off to visit the sick, taking her husband with her.

Maisie sat in front of the fire enjoying the unexpected luxury of solitude. Occasionally she sniffed and blew her nose but she would have denied that she was suffering from coryza. By the time Peter came home from his evening classes, however, all trace of her handkerchief work was gone—or so she thought.

Peter, with youthful enthusiasm, emphasised his return by banging the kitchen door.

'Oh, for goodness sake,' whispered Maisie fiercely, 'keep quiet! Ian's sleeping. We don't want him to waken up, and have to answer another five thousand of his questions.'

'Is he in my bed?'

'No, he insisted on being put in Matt's room—said it wasn't healthy for two people to sleep in the same bed.'

37

'You're kidding!'

'I'm not!'

Peter peered closer at his sister and said bluntly that she was looking a bit under the weather. This she denied vehemently, so vehemently that he implored her not to part with her hair, that he was not begging for confidences, and finally, had she been reading any good books lately? She got up and went into the scullery, banging the door and telling him to leave her alone.

'Here you,' he shouted, 'make less noise! You'll waken the kid!'

She opened the door to inform him that the scullery door could not possibly be heard at the distance of Matt's room, banging it again by way of illustration. Peter stared at it and yelled:

'What are you doing in there anyway—making the supper? Weren't you out with Jim tonight?'

Again the door was opened. 'I'm washing my stockings,' she said, and once again there was a slam.

'Don't bang that door!' shouted Peter.

The retort came through the quickly opened door: 'The kid's more likely to hear you yelling your head off. Pipe down!' By way of an exclamation mark, she slammed the door again.

'If Jim and you have quarrelled you don't need to take it out on me!' complained the lad at the top of his voice.

In a moment she stood before him: 'I have not quarrelled with Jim. And I am not discussing the matter!' And in the next moment she was behind the door again with more expression than ever.

'H-uh! Temper!' roared Peter. 'You need to practise self-control! The lecturer was saying at the psychology class the other night that temper and lack of self-control were the result of a maladjustment——'

His verbatim report was rudely interrupted. 'And I do not want to be lectured! If I feel in need of some psychological advice I'll go where I'll get it properly cooked and not the half-baked rubbish you talk !' And away she went again with another explosion of wood.

'Right you are !' called back Peter, 'but the sooner you go for it the better. You're looking like something the cat refused to bring in.'

'Nobody asked for your opinion !' She came out once again but stayed longer this time. 'And anyway, you're the last one that should talk about looks ! If I had a face like yours I wouldn't be trusted with a gas-oven.'

'If you had a face like mine you'd be in a side-show !'

'Huh—think you're funny—you and your cheap jokes and your elementary psychology and your pale-pink politics——'

'Politics !' Peter leapt at the word like a cock at a grosset. ' If you'd take the time to think for yourself——'

'Think ? What thinking have you ever done ? You just lap up the first spoon-fed second-hand half-baked rubbish——'

'You're repeating yourself, Maisie. I've told you before, in a properly organised state of society——'

'Yes !' she blazed. 'You've told me before—hundreds of times !'

'Oh, for the luva mike let me finish what I was saying ! The fact is you're narrow-minded and conventional and——'

'What ! Me—narrow-minded ? It's because you haven't the intelligence to appreciate intelligence !'

'Don't kid yourself, Maisie ! You're not intelligent— you're a teacher !'

'Huh—more of your cheap jokes !'

'It's not a cheap joke—it's a recognised fact ! You teachers seem to think that because you've got a university degree you're the fount of all wisdom, so you shut your minds to all new ideas. As a class, teachers are bigoted and self-opinionated and——'

But she had had enough. She swept into the scullery again and closed the door very thoroughly. Peter, however, was not to be silenced so easily. He raised his voice once more : ' Because you spend all day standing on your hind legs laying down the law to a crowd of kids, you think you can come home and do the same thing. I'm fed up being treated like a school kid.'

The door opened, but not the scullery one, and Ian's piping little voice asked why Uncle Peter was shouting. The sound of it reached Maisie, who was in their presence in a moment.

'There you are, Peter! I told you you were shouting too much. Serve you right!'

But Ian, in the interests of truth, stated that it was not shouting that had wakened him but the banging of a door. 'I want a piece!' he added.

'What did I tell you, Maisie? You've got a fiend of a temper.'

'I have *not* got the fiend of a temper! But you and your soap-box oratory would drive a saint mad.'

'It's not soap-box oratory, it's . . .' and he broke off suddenly for another sound had reached his ears, that of his parents returning from their call on Mrs McLeather. He shook off Ian, who was repeating his demand for a 'piece,' and edged nearer his sister. 'Look here, Maisie, the sooner you stop treating me like a school kid——'

'I'll stop treating you like a school kid as soon as you stop acting like one.'

At that their mother rushed on to the stage. 'Ian!' she demanded. 'What are you doing out of bed—and standing on the floor with your bare feet!'

'I want a piece. I'm hungry!'

Upon which Willie, coming on the scene, spoke a few lines on his own instigation. 'Here, you two—what are ye thinkin' aboot tae let the wean catch 'is daith o' cauld?'

'Oh, he hasn't been standing there a minute, Dad!' said Maisie.

'I've been standing here for hours and hours,' said the child, 'only you and Uncle Peter were shouting so much you didn't see me.'

'That's right,' said Sarah, 'we could hear the row when we were coming up the stair.'

'Gran, I'm hungry. I want a piece. I don't like being wakened because doors are banging.'

'Oh, you wee clype,' said Maisie none too affectionately.

'Maisie ! What a thing to say !' exclaimed Sarah.

'Yes !' jeered Peter, 'and her a teacher !'

'Will you shut your trap !' Maisie's face was transfixed with rage so that they all gaped at her. 'I'm fed to the teeth with you. See—let me past. I'm going to bed.'

'Maisie !' Sarah reached out a hand to stop the girl, but without success. 'You're not going without your supper !'

The only answer was the closing of the door with even more expression than hitherto.

'Oh dear-dear,' wailed Sarah, 'that's terrible. Peter—what have you been saying to her ?'

While Peter was in the midst of his denial that he had said anything to offend her, Ian was clutching at his grandmother's skirts, clamouring for a 'piece.'

'All right. Here's a biscuit.' And she reached towards the tin kept for the purpose.

'A biscuit isn't a piece !' said the child.

'Gie'm a double decker, Serah,' said Willie, meaning a smear of jam between two half slices of bread, but the small boy refused to have anything to do with it.

'All-right, all-right !' said the harassed grandmother. 'Peter —away you go and get his dressing-gown and slippers and bring them in here.' And while Peter went off obediently she added, 'I'd better give Ian some hot milk in case he gets the cold.'

'Mummy says hot milk isn't good for me.'

'You'll take whit yer gran gies ye, my lad,' said Willie. 'We've hin enough o' whit yer mammy says this last coupla days !' From which we may gather that Polly did not number her father among her admirers.

'My mummy knows better'n emb'dy else 'cept my daddy !' said Ian firmly.

The matter was dropped while the child followed Sarah into the scullery and saw her spread some butter on a slice of fruit bread. When he learnt that it was intended for him he declined it in favour of plain bread and jam, which he insisted on having ;

then, when he was finally presented with this 'piece,' he complained that he did not care for raspberry jam. Willie asked if the reason for this was that the seeds got below his false plate. After that the child's demands were querulous with drowsiness.

He wanted a chocolate biscuit, he did not want a chocolate biscuit. He wanted a drink, he did not want a drink of warm milk. He wanted to go to bed, he did not want to go to bed before his Uncle Peter had also retired. In exasperation Willie ordered his son to bed immediately, but before Peter could open his mouth in protest Ian was wailing that he wanted to go home.

Willie tried coaxing. 'Heh, Ian, wid ye no' like tae sleep wi' yer Uncle Peter? It wid be cheerier fur ye.'

'No. My mummy says it isn't healthy.'

'Ach, haud ma hauns aff'm, somebody!' pleaded Willie.

'I tell you what, Ian,' said Peter, 'if you drink your milk and eat this biscuit, I'll come and tell you a story after you're in bed.'

'What kind of story?'

Sarah suggested that Peter might recount the narrative of the three bears, but this was turned down on the ground of being a girl's story.

'Well,' Peter tried again, 'I could tell you a story about a wee boy called——'

'Ian?' queried the child, intrigued into amiability.

'Could be.'

So in a moment or two, having swallowed the milk in large gulps, Ian allowed himself to be led away by Peter, who lured him on with a tale about a snowstorm that had made the world look as if somebody, with a great big sugar-sifter, had sprinkled the world with icing sugar.

2

About two o'clock in the morning Ian, turning himself over in his sleep, was wakened by a peculiar noise overhead. Since his home in Edinburgh was a bungalow, he was alarmed at the strangeness of the direction and called out in terror. In a moment or two his grandmother was with him. Before going to bed she had opened the bedroom door as well as the door of the kitchen wherein she and Willie slept, in the event of just such an emergency. She switched on the light.

'Were you frightened of the dark, sonny?' she asked.

'I heard a funny noise. Where's Mummy?'

'Your mummy's in Edinburgh, Ian. D'you not remember you're staying with Gran in Glasgow? For a wee holiday?'

'Yes.'

'You've been dreaming, poor wee man!'

'I wasn't dreaming. I heard a noise.'

'Never mind about it now. Lie over a bit and Gran'll come in beside you.'

'No. Mummy says it isn't healthy. I'm not frightened any more. Tell me a story, Gran.'

'I'm afraid I only know girls' stories,' she confessed. 'Did your Uncle Peter tell you a nice story?'

'Yes,' said the child in happy reminiscence. 'It was about a wee boy called Ian.' And in the retelling of the story he fell asleep. Sarah crept away leaving the light burning.

An hour later he was wakened again by the same sound from the same extraordinary direction, and again he screamed, 'Gran!'

Normally Peter slept heavily, but for some reason he was sufficiently alive to his surroundings to hear the plaintive cry. He got to the spare bedroom first. 'Hullo-hullo-hullo! What's all this shouting about? Why's the light on?' he asked light-heartedly.

'Oh, Uncle Peter, I'm frightened. It's the noise again!'

'What noise? I don't hear anything!' He cupped his hands over his ear like an old man, by way of illustration.

At that the grandfather came on the scene, and he too cupped his hands over his ears and insisted he could hear nothing. He said, 'Ye musta been dreamin', son!'

Ian was indignant. 'I wasn't dreaming. It wakened me. I'm frightened.'

Sarah, dominant in her dressing-gown, swept into the room.

' See here, Ian, we can't have this. I don't care what your mummy says. I'm coming in beside you. Peter—away you back to your bed. You, too, Willie.'

' But I don't want anybody in the bed beside me. I want to know what the noise is.'

' There's nae noise, son. Listen ! '

They all listened to the silence.

' There you are—see ! ' said the grandmother.

' But there *was* a noise. Like this ! ' and the child tried to imitate something he had no parallel for.

' Get away with you, Ian,' said his uncle, ' there's no such noise ! '

' But there was ! ' he almost shrieked. ' I heard it ! Up in the roof there ! '

' That's not the roof, son ! ' said Sarah as patiently as she could considering the hour. ' There's another house above this one. You've always been used with a bungalow.'

' Listen ! ' yelled the child, his eyes wide with terror. ' There it is again ! '

' Whit the bleezes ! ' began Willie as the most unearthly sound seemed to trundle over their heads. Peter gaped at his mother.

' I thought you said the McMuslins were away just now.'

' Mr McMuslin is, but she's at home.'

' D'ye no' think ye'd be better tae away up an' see if there's onything wrang ? ' asked Willie, appointing a delegate in the person of his wife.

' I will not ! ' snapped Sarah. ' Mrs McMuslin hasn't looked at me for years—too high and mighty she's got ! '

' Oh, but Mother,' said Peter, ' if there's some kind of trouble. Burglars, for instance ! '

That took some of the starch out of the woman. ' Oh, I never thought of burglars ! What about you and your father going up to see ? '

' Me, too, Gran,' came the voice from the bed, ' I want to see burglars ! '

' You'll stay where you are ! ' was the retort. ' I tell you what we'll do. Peter—you go and waken Maisie and tell her to get up and look after Ian, and the three of us, you and your father and me'll go upstairs.'

'Okay!' Peter went off to oblige, knocking at Maisie's door in complete forgetfulness of the unpleasant words that had passed between them earlier in the night. She seemed to be awake, for she replied immediately, although in somewhat muffled tones, that he was to go away and leave her alone.

'Good grief!' he called back. 'Are you still in the huff?'

Leaving the scene without further ado, he went back to the spare bedroom. Some unfathomed deep in his nature kept him from reporting the full facts to his mother; all he said was that Maisie did not feel like being disturbed, and that he would stay and look after Ian.

Ian took a good deal of man-handling before he was prevented from accompanying the reconnaissance party. With their overcoats on top of their night-clothes, Willie and Sarah mounted the stairs. The door-bell seemed to echo throughout the whole tenement. Sarah shuddered and said she wouldn't like to be wakened out of her sleep with a noise like that.

'Cheer up!' whispered Willie dramatically, 'maybe she wisnae sleepin'. Maybe thon noise wis hur gettin' rowed aboot on the flair bein' murdered!'

'Willie—don't be vulgar—at this time of night!'

After a long wait during which they were reluctant to pull the old-fashioned bell again, they heard footsteps approaching and Mrs McMuslin's voice calling from the other side of the door:

'Who is it?'

'It's me—Mrs McFlannel!' said Sarah, adding, 'and Mr McFlannel.'

Judging by the number of snibs and bolts that were thereupon manipulated, Mrs McMuslin had little trust in human nature. Eventually, however, the door was opened and she peered round asking:

'What's the matter? Burst pipes?'

'Naw,' said Willie, 'it's jist we wur kinna worried aboot

whether ye were safe enough wi' that noise goin' on in yer hoose.'

' What noise ? I heard nothing.'

' Yes,' said Sarah, ' it's above our spare bedroom. Our wee grandson wakened up with it.'

' He must have been dreaming ! ' The lady appeared to withdraw her head as if in dismissal. ' I'm alone in the house.'

' Oh, but we heard it too ! ' insisted Sarah.

Willie said : ' That's right, missus. It wis like this ! ' And he in turn tried to imitate the sound, without, we fear, any more verisimilitude than his grandson.

' Ridiculous ! There's no such noise. Which room did you say ? '

' The bedroom at the front.'

' Well, whatever the noise was, I can assure you it wasn't coming from that room. It's been shut and locked for months.'

With mischievous intent and because he was exasperated by the woman's aloofness, Willie bent nearer the narrow opening and whispered : ' Maybe it's a ghost ! '

' Don't be stupid. And now, if you'll excuse me . . .'

' Oh, but Mrs McMuslin ! ' pleaded Sarah with outstretched hand to prevent the closing of the door, ' maybe it's burglars ! '

There was a sneering giggle in the darkness. ' I shouldn't imagine burglars would make enough noise to waken a child ! '

' Well,' said Willie, ' we a' heard somethin' gey queer. Wid ye like me tae get a polisman fur ye, seein' yer man's no' at hame ? '

' No ! I should very much prefer to be left alone. Goodnight ! '

The door was almost closed, when Sarah suddenly shrieked : ' Listen—there it is again ! '

' Good gracious ! It's coming from that bedroom ! ' In her amazement Mrs McMuslin opened the door wide and revealed herself as dressed in a flimsy dressing-gown.

' Wid ye like me tae look an' see, missus, in case it's——'

' There's no light in that room ! ' The woman's voice shook with superstitious terror.

46

'Ach, it's a braw bricht munelicht nicht. Will Ah come in ?'

The request seemed hardly necessary for he was already over the threshold, his wife at his heels. With the stair gas as his only illumination, Willie tiptoed, for some unknown reason, in the direction of the mysterious room. Mrs McMuslin, unable to speak, pointed to the key in the lock. Willie turned it and stealthily opened the door, peering in.

'Jeengs, the room's as emp'y as the Sahara desert,' and his wife was too intent on trying not to be frightened by swatches of moonlight on a bare-boarded floor to notice the expression on the face of her neighbour. Flinging the door wide, the man strode into the room.

'Help ma boab !' he exclaimed. 'It's a cat—a kitten. An' it's been playing' wi' a gless ba'.'

Mrs McMuslin swallowed hard before saying : 'Oh, it's a glass ball from the grate. But how could the cat have got in ?'

'Yer windae's open !' said Willie. 'An' there's a ledge rins alang ablow it tae the next hoose. Ah've often noticed that ledge an' said tae masel' . . .'

The animal, not at all frightened, came daintily forward and Sarah recognised it as belonging to Mrs McMuslin's neighbour ; the lady, however, did not thank her for the information. Instead she moved towards her outer door, and with the air of a third-rate tragedy queen held it open saying :

'Well now, perhaps, having satisfied your curiosity, you'll take yourselves *and* the cat away.'

Sarah was deeply hurt by both the manner and the speech. 'We were only trying to help you !' she said in the bye-going.

'So *you* say !'

Murmuring shame-faced and self-pitying 'goodnights' man and wife crept down the stairs, deciding not to disturb any more of their neighbours by returning the cat to its home.

'Who does she think she is anyway ?' demanded Sarah in her wrath.

'Ach, maybe she wis mad at gettin' waukened oota 'er sleep. Ye're whiles kinna crabbit yersel' when ye're waukened wi' a stert.'

Peter met them at the door, gaped at the cat and listened with a satisfying amazement to the tale. While Willie went off to let Ian see the animal after first making sure that the kitchen door was closed on Susan's suspicions, Peter prodded his mother for further information.

'But I don't understand how there was all that noise if there was a carpet on the floor.'

'There was no carpet, Peter! No furniture! Nothing! And the nippiness of her! Fancy giving herself such airs—and her with an unfurnished room in her house!'

'Maybe that's why she was nippy—defence mechanism, you know?' said the amateur psychologist.

'Oh, I could do with a cup of tea!'

'I've got the kettle on,' said he. 'I tell you what—if you make it, I'll knock at Maisie's door and ask her if she'd like a cup. I don't think she's feeling well.'

Too exhausted emotionally to take in the last sentence, Sarah went off to the kitchen, while Peter knocked once again on his sister's door.

'Go away,' she called.

He opened the door and went in, gaping all over again, this time at the spectacle of the girl sitting, fully clothed, at her bedside.

'I said—go away!' she stormed.

'Sorry. I thought you said Okay!' he replied, just a thought too glibly. Going over to her and touching her shoulder with the awkwardness of a younger brother, he wheedled: 'Maisie, will you not tell me what's up? Was it—I mean—I'm sorry if I hurt your feelings with what I said about you—being a teacher.'

'Oh, forget it,' she shrugged.

'Come on, old girl. Cough it up!' he persisted.

'Oh, don't pester me!'

'I'm not pestering you. I only want to give you the loan of my shoulder if you're needing it for crying on to. Maisie'—he paused—'if—I mean—if somebody's hurt you, I'll—ugh, go on, tell me.'

48

Maisie unwrapped a moist ball of cloth that had started life as a handkerchief, mopped her eyes with it and said, ' Oh, Peter, don't be kind to me. I can't stand it ! '

' Here—take my hankie,' he said, pulling a fresh one from the pocket of his dressing-gown. ' That one of yours is looking a bit under the weather.'

' Oh, Peter,' she sobbed from the shelter of the luxurious cambric, ' it's Jim ! He doesn't—lul—like me any more.'

' How d'you know ? Did he tell you ? '

' Well, he never wants to make a date with me now ! '

' But I didn't think you were particularly struck on him ! '

' Neither I was. It was only when he—he lost interest in me that I—I realised how I felt about him. Oh, Peter, I'm silly to be telling you all this.'

' No, you're not ! You know it's safe with me anyway ! '

' I know.' She reached up a hand to the one on her shoulder and patted it. It was easier, somehow, to talk to him when he was standing behind her like that.

' I never liked to tell you before, Maisie, but I couldn't bear the chap—that arty-crafty way of speaking gets my goat. Whatever did you see in him ? '

' I dud—don't know nun—now ! ' She wheeled round to face him. ' You won't tell Mother or Dad ? '

' Cross-my-heart-and-hope-to-die ! '

At that the door was pushed open and their mother came in carrying a cup of tea.

' Maisie ! ' she exclaimed, ' have you been crying ? '

Peter sprang to the rescue. ' She had something in her eye, Mum, but I've taken it out.'

' Oh ! ' She laid the tea on the bedside table, saying : ' Well, drink up your tea or you'll be sleeping-in in the morning.'

' Thanks, Mother. Goodnight,' said Maisie.

' Goodnight.' Sarah made for the door saying that she would need to see wee Ian tucked up for the night.

Alone again together, Maisie smiled and said : ' Thanks for the brave lie, Peter.'

' It wasn't a lie. At least not altogether. There was a tear in your eye when I came in, but I think it's gone now.'

' I believe it is,' she sniffed. ' Well, goodnight—and thanks for the loan of your shoulder.'

' Oh, that's all right. I'm keeping the other one in reserve for future eventualities.'

Chapter 5

HAM-AND-EGG TEA

The following week, Ian being once again in the bosom of his parents, a letter arrived from Matt announcing that he would be having three weeks at home while his ship was laid up for repair at a Clyde shipyard. As usual, the news sent his mother into a fluster of preparations none of which penetrated the sailor's consciousness ; and on this occasion he turned out to be even less aware than usual of his surroundings. After several false starts he eventually admitted that his thoughts were else-where, and, on being pressed for details, said that the subject of his preoccupation was called Ella McSatin, and that her father had been in the same Home Guard unit as ex-sergeant William McFlannel D.C.M. Trying not to show that she was hurt at the casual way in which her favourite had had to have the informa-tion dragged out of him, Sarah asked if he were engaged to the girl, and her feelings were not soothed when he told her that there had been an understanding between them since his last leave, and that they intended exchanging engagement rings within the next day or two.

'When are ye bringin' 'er up tae the hoose ? ' asked Willie.

'Oh well,' said Matt diffidently, 'just as soon as she gets an invitation.'

'Goodness, Matt ! ' exclaimed his mother, ' you know you're welcome to bring her as soon as she likes to come.'

'That's not good enough, Mother ! ' put in Maisie. ' You'll need to fix a definite date.'

The sailor threw his sister a grateful look. ' It looks as if you've been through the mill yourself, eh ? '

'Them as axes no questions is told no lies,' was the girl's off-hand answer, to which her mother, striving to hide her hurt feelings, retorted :

'Maisie, what grammar—and you a teacher !'

Hooting with laughter, Peter turned his mother's thoughts in another direction by suggesting that they could fix the reception for the following evening—since he would be absent at a class. When he had been reprimanded for such anti-social propensities, the five of them laid their heads together, finally emerging from the scrum without any decision as to the date.

'Mind,' said Willie, 'it's tae be a ham-an'-egg tea. It's no' a right engagement unless.'

'We will not !' interjected his wife. 'It's common !'

'Common ?' repeated Willie in astonishment. 'It's that *un*common thae days that Ah havenae hin a decent feed o't since afore the war.'

Seeing the distress on his mother's face Matt assured her that Ella would not expect anything special, but Maisie reminded him that unless ham and egg were offered, their father would refuse to recognise the engagement as official.

'Who's your " official " just now, Maisie ?' asked Matt.

'Oh, I'm having a wee bawrley.'

Sarah was aghast at the expression. 'Maisie ! Where do you pick up vulgar words like that ?' she demanded.

'Yes !' Peter sided with his mother ostensibly. 'And you a teacher, Maisie !'

The banter continued until the practical Sarah asked for a description of the prospective daughter-in-law, and while they all hung on his words, Matt stammered, 'Oh she's—well—I—she's sort of—oh, you know—ehm . . .'

As though to help him out Sarah said, 'What kind of house does she live in ?'

Once again Matt sought in vain for the right words. 'Oh, an ordinary sort of house. A flat.'

'A flat ?' repeated his mother. 'You mean—like this ?'

'Well—sort of.'

'Oh, I'm awful glad. I don't know how it was—maybe with

you being an officer and all that—I got the idea she'd maybe be
—well, kind of swanky.'

Matt laid a reassuring hand on his mother's arm : ' You've
got nothing to be frightened of with Ella. She's as natural as
you are yourself.'

Which comforted Sarah somewhat, but Maisie seemed to
have lingering suspicions, for she asked what Ella did for a living.
Matt hesitating, Peter urged :

' Tell us quick, Matt. But don't tell us she's a teacher ! '

Since the teaching profession in Sarah's eyes was the highest
to which one could attain, she demanded to know what was
wrong with it in the eyes of her younger son, who retorted that
one of the species in the family was enough.

' *Is* she a teacher ? ' demanded Maisie, dusting her hands after
woman-handling the lad.

' Well—sort of.' Matt's reticence was embarrassing to all
except Peter, who exclaimed, ' Suffering saints ! '

' I mean,' went on Matt uncomfortably, ' she's not an ordinary
day-school teacher like Maisie. She's—she's got something to
do with speech and that sort of thing.'

' Oh, an elocutionist ? ' asked Maisie with a faint suggestion
of patronising interest.

Matt's overworked ' Well—sort of ' called forth Peter's
query as to the ability of his prospective sister-in-law to recite
' The Green Eye of the Little Yellow God.'

' Oh, I hope she can,' said Sarah. ' I like that piece. We
must get her to say it when she comes up.'

' Only over my dead body ! '

' Oh, Peter ! ' said his mother, ' that's an awful-like thing to
say about Matt's girl.'

An argument might have developed on the subject of
individual aesthetic tastes, but Maisie saved the situation by asking
if Matt thought his fiancée could do anything about their father's
speech.

' Oh, Dad's fine,' said Matt, who clearly wanted to be left
in peace, but his ejaculation had been heard with pleasure in
one quarter.

'Say that again, Matt!' shouted Willie. 'Say it oot lood so's Maisie an' Peter can hear ye. They're aye on at me——'

'But, Matt,' put in Sarah, 'if Ella's an elocution teacher will she not laugh at people for the way they speak?'

'Listen, Mother—Ella's the nicest girl you've ever met. She's not in the least affected or stuck up. When'll I ask her to come and see you?' Matt ended up rather breathlessly.

'Well, if Peter's going out tomorrow night—what about the night after?'

Maisie volunteering the information that the suggested date was okay by her, Peter added :

'It's okay by me too—worse luck!' Then, in a sepulchral tone he went on, ' " There's a broken-hearted woman in the State of Khatmandu. . . ." '

Ignoring the dramatic interlude, Willie said, ' She's tae come fur 'er tea, mind.'

To his mother's consternation Matt rose and said he'd just take a run-over and see Ella. It was impossible for Sarah to hide her feelings, and she urged :

'But you're just home, Matt, and—well—Ella will be having you for the rest of her life.'

'Come on, Mother,' said Maisie, sensing the atmosphere of tension and making her brother grateful to her, ' don't act the heavy mother-in-law.'

For a moment it looked as if Sarah was going to weep, but suddenly she squared her mental shoulders and asked if it would be all right to have tea in the kitchen.

'Of course!' said Matt, relieved. ' I want you to treat Ella just like one of the family.'

'Well, here, Matt,' said Willie, ' tell the lassie no' to take much dinner that day, so's she'll hae a guid appetite fur a guid tuck-in o' ham an' egg.'

While the commissariat discussed the possibility of the ritual meal being served Matt made his escape. Just as he was closing the door, however, Peter called after him :

'If you like, I'll lend you my photo of me with nothing on but my birthday suit,' a remark that had to be explained to the bewildered navyman. ' Mother's sure to want to tell Ella what a nice baby you were. So she can show her my photo. Ella won't know the difference.'

Matt came back into the kitchen with a bound. ' Mother, if you go and show Ella any photos of me as a kid. . . .' His threat died away for lack of punishment to fit the crime.

' Why not ? ' Sarah asked innocently. ' I'm sure the girl would be quite pleased.'

This had the effect of bringing Matt to the fireside in such indignation that Peter had to assure him that he would be responsible for the safe hiding of the family album. Matt was not yet easy in his mind, however, for he insisted that he would be most annoyed if Ella were shown any photographs of him wearing a sailor suit.

' An' whit-fur no' ? ' demanded his father. ' The lassie never sees ye in onythin' else bar a sailor suit thae days.'

With a few further instructions tossed to his brother and sister, Matt left the house, leaving the rest to settle with Sarah the ultimate fate of these records of their youthful indiscretions. Sarah, for her part, was obviously not greatly concerned with the fate of the album, and it was with some difficulty that her husband managed to extract from her the confession that something else was worrying her, namely the propriety of serving a meal in the kitchen. ' What sort of man is Ella's father ? ' she asked.

Willie scratched his head to assist recollection. ' Ach, he's jist an ordinary man like masel,' he conceded at length ; adding, in reply to a direct question from Peter, ' Well, maybe he disnae speak jist as plain as me. Ye'd think he had a cheugh jean in 'is mooth a' the time.'

Sarah was still uneasy though. ' What does he work at ? ' she asked.

Once again Willie sought for inspiration with the tips of his fingers. ' Hoo should Ah know ? Ah don't think he works at onythin'.'

' You mean—he's unemployed ? '

Conscious that he was evading the point, Willie took refuge

in ' Hoo should Ah know ? ' for the second time. Then, as a sop to his conscience, ' We were never awful pally.'

Unaware of the mental reservations that guarded her husband's replies, Sarah sighed with relief and said :

' Oh, well, if the girl's father's not working, she'll maybe be glad of a good square meal. I think I *will* have ham and eggs after all—in the kitchen.'

The family exchanged tolerant smiles.

On the appropriate night Maisie rushed home from school, panting her apologies for being kept late at a staff meeting. She found her mother surprisingly calm.

' Your father and Peter are in the sitting-room all ready waiting,' she said. ' Matt and Ella should be here any minute now. Away you and get washed—and mind and leave the hand-basin clean ! '

On her way to obey instructions Maisie's eyes were caught by the spectacle of the family washing draped from the pulleys at the ceiling. In view of the near approach of the state visitor she protested.

' I couldn't get the things dried outside today,' was her mother's defence. ' And anyway they're mostly Matt's things.'

' But, Mother, they spoil the look of the kitchen ! '

' Now, Maisie, don't make a fuss,' was the reply. ' The girl's bound to have seen a washing on a pulley manys a time if her father's out of a job. Besides, she'll have to wash Matt's clothes herself some day."

' Still, Mother, what's the use of being proud of an interior grate and a bed-settee in your kitchen if you're going to ruin the dining-room effect by draping Matt's pants all over the place ? '

' They're not all pants and they're not all over the place ! ' exclaimed Sarah indignantly. ' If Ella's father's not working she'll think this is a palace. Now away you go and——'

' But, Mother——' began the girl, when her father drowned her protest by appearing on the scene complaining that there was no sign of the young couple, and that as a result his stomach was under the impression that his throat was cut. Maisie left her

mother to deal with the situation, which was done by assuring
the hungry man that the ham was already cooked and that the
eggs would be put in the pan as soon as Matt and Ella arrived.
Willie surveyed the frying-pan, licking his chops and commenting
favourably on the farm-house size scones which were in course
of cooking in the ham grease.

' I want the girl to feel at home,' explained Sarah. ' She'll
may be hungry, poor thing.'

Silencing his misgivings, the man remarked that it was un-
usual not to have ' double knives ' for high tea.

' Oh well, I thought she might be embarrassed if we showed
too much grandeur all at once. We can teach her gradually.
That is—if she isn't another Ivy McTweed.'

' A' the same, ye michta been better . . .' began Willie,
but his belated honesty was choked by the sound of the
door-bell.

' Oh, there they are ! ' exclaimed Sarah. ' Now mind—you
take Matt into the sitting-room and I'll take Ella into Matt's
room to take off her things. It's not so fancy as Maisie's.' Dragging the reluctant host in the direction of the door she asked in
a fierce whisper if he had remembered to put a clean handkerchief
in his pocket.

' It's not ma nose that's botherin' me,' he replied without the
token modesty of a whisper. ' It's ma bel—stummuck.'

The introductions were performed in a confusion of embarrassment on Matt's part, in hungry desperation on Willie's
part, in surprise at the girl's calmness on Sarah's part, and in
keyhole alertness on the part of Maisie, who was still in the
bathroom. Willie, as he had been told, conducted Matt to
the sitting-room, flinging over his shoulder the reminder that the
visitor had come for tea, not for album inspection. His pleasantry
had the direct result of reminding Sarah that she had hidden
the album in a box below Matt's bed, and the visitor, unaware of
the necessity for speed in serving the meal, aided and abetted in the
inspection. She exclaimed pleasantly at the picture of Matt in
his first sailor suit at the age of four and a half. Thus encouraged
Sarah went on :

'And here's another one—in a kilt. I got the loan of it from a neighbour who'd a wee boy the same age.'

'The darling!' said Ella. 'Doesn't he look terribly apologetic! Is the kilt breaking away from its moorings, or is it meant to be like that?'

'Well, maybe it *was* a wee bit big for him. He's terribly ashamed of that photo. And look—here's Peter when he was six months old. He'd be awful angry if he knew I showed it to you.'

'No wonder! The poor mite's not even wearing a smile.'

When unflattering and archaic impressions had been shown of all the family, Sarah turned to the girl sympathetically and asked if she was very excited about the ordeal of coming to meet her prospective in-laws.

'Well, I was a bit at first,' admitted the girl. 'But Matt's told me so much about you all—you especially, that—well—I was just wearying to meet you.' Sarah blinked and swallowed hard, the thought flashing through her mind that this girl might be poor but she had nicer instincts than Peter's ex-girl-friend, Ivy McTweed. 'And whenever I saw you,' continued Ella in her attractive voice, 'I don't know what happened to me but I felt—oh, I don't know how to put it into words—I felt you were just the kind of mother I'd 've liked to have myself.'

'Fancy that!' was all Sarah could say.

'I lost my mother when I was a baby, you know.'

'Oh, you poor wee soul! And you had to go and live with relatives?'

'No. Daddy got a nurse for me, and then when I was old enough I went to a boarding-school, but even there it was pretty bad, for the other girls used to talk so much about their mummies and they'd get letters from them too! I used to feel horribly sorry for myself, you know.'

Sarah struggled for speech. 'You—you went to a boarding-school?'

'Yes—in St Andrews.'

'Thuth-then what happened that your father's not working now?'

'Oh, Dad never worked in his life, poor lamb! He couldn't

bear life in the country so he's let the estate to a cotton manu-
facturer and we're living in town.'

'B-but Matt said you lived up a close like us—in
a three-room-and-kitchen, I thought.' When the girl seemed
bewildered, Sarah went on : 'Is it not a house like this ? '

Ella licked dry lips. 'Well, we live in a flat and my brother's
room isn't unlike this one—he and Matt have that in common—
they're both untidy.' Trying to make amends, she went on :
'In fact I'm sure Hamish's room is a lot more untidy than this
one. You should hear what the housekeeper has to say about it.'

'You've got a housekeeper ? ' gasped Sarah. 'Huh-have you
a car as well ? '

'Yes, both Dad and Hamish have a car, but please, Mrs
McFlannel, don't think any less of me because I'm not what you
thought I was. I thought we were going to be such good friends,
and now you're looking at me as if we were strangers ! '

The shrewd assessment of her attitude shook Sarah and she
was about to protest when her husband came suddenly on the
scene, shouting that he was famishing.

Conscience-stricken and ill at ease in the presence of this
invasion from another social sphere, Sarah bustled the girl out
of the bedroom and into the sitting-room where she introduced
Peter, and got confused in her worry about whether she had
got the names in their right order. Ella, however, put everyone
at their ease by saying to Peter that she believed she was going
to be a disappointment to him.

'How ? ' demanded the bewildered Sarah.

'Don't tell me you can't say "The Green Eye of the Little
Yellow God " ! ' exclaimed Peter in mock dejection.

Sarah left the room as the girl replied that she could not
get beyond 'There's a broken-hearted woman in the something
of Katmandu.' Shutting the door on the recital, Sarah rushed
to the kitchen where Maisie had gone.

'You'll never guess what's happened ? ' she panted. 'Matt's
girl ! '

Maisie, tea-caddy in hand, asked calmly if the damsel had
crinkly hair and too much of the sun.

'She's gentry!' wailed the distraught mother. 'Servants and cars and boarding-schools and all that. I knew whenever she opened her mouth she was a lady but I thought it was all put on like these elocutionists do. Maisie!' She laid a restraining hand on the arm that hugged the tea-caddy. 'We can't bring her into the kitchen here and give her anything as common as ham and egg!'

Maisie agreed, adding that Matt's neathies on the pulley did nothing to raise the tone of the apartment.

'That settles it!' said Sarah. 'We'll need to take the tea into the sitting-room. On the trolley. Quick. We'll need to make sandwiches.'

'And Dad crying out loud for ham and egg?' asked Maisie.

'It can't be helped. Look—you cream this quarter of margarine and I'll grate some cheese and we'll mix them together —it'll be quicker to spread than anything else and we can half the morning rolls to make them look daintier.'

Maisie proved awkward and for the sake of urgency her mother took over the job herself, moaning, 'Oh, isn't this terrible! Thank goodness the best china's in the sitting-room press and it's clean!'

Working as quickly as they knew how, Maisie and her mother commiserated with each other on this new acquisition to the family circle. 'Is she awfully " wally-close-gless-door " ? ' asked the girl.

'Maisie, I do wish you wouldn't speak like that! She's got a lovely voice. I feel I could listen to it for hours.'

'I can't wait to see the paragon,' was the retort. 'What are her clothes like? Straight from Paris?'

'Not a bit of it! Very quiet—in fact, I couldn't tell you what she was wearing.'

'Sounds like Paris all right. Commend me to the McFlannel sons for picking up queer birds. I hope Matt hasn't a disappointment coming to him after she's seen us.'

'She'd on a huge bangle. . . . Oh dear, this margarine's hard! I'm sure it's solid gold!'

'What? The marge?'

'No—her bangle ! How are you getting on with the cheese ? '

Maisie's punning reply was not received with much hilarity, so she carried it a point further by admitting that she appeared to be grating on her mother too. But by that time Sarah was away in a realm of her own :

'I tell you what, Maisie. You wheel in the trolley and set the cups and saucers on it and that'll take up their attention for a wee bit.'

Maisie made a move to comply ; but murmuring that she still thought cheese sandwiches a poor substitute for ham and egg, she added, ' What Dad'll say won't be for publication.'

'Oh, but wait till you see the girl, Maisie ! You'll realise she's never eaten anything so common as ham and egg in her life. How Matt managed to catch her I don't know. He's good-looking, of course. I'm not sure but what I'd've been more at home with Ivy McTweed.'

With a formal ' Come on, Mother, you don't mean that,' Maisie trundled the trolley out of the kitchen. Just as she reached the door of the sitting-room it was opened and her father almost fell over her vehicle in his anxiety to ask if she had come to announce the service of the meal. Maisie, however, kept pushing until she had reached the centre of the room.

'Ella, this is my wee sister Maisie,' said Matt.

The two girls made acknowledgment with a cautious ' How d'you do ! ' and while they were still eyeing each other Peter declared his disgust at the fraud that had been perpetrated on him owing to the visitor's inability to recite traditional epics. Cutting into the midst of this inanity Willie demanded :

'Are we to go ben noo, Maisie ? Ah'm like tae drap wi' hung-er.'

'Half a mo', Dad,' commanded Maisie as calmly as she knew how, ' till I get the dishes set on the trolley.'

'But the tea wis set hauf an hour ago in the kitchen. Ah seen it ! '

'I know—I know, but Mother has changed her plans. She'll be here in a minute.'

'But whit aboot wur ham an' egg?' demanded the man heartrendingly.

'I told you—Mother has changed her plans. We're having cheese sandwiches.'

Yelling 'Cheese sangwidges!' the man rushed from the room and his protests came spurting back to them as he reached the kitchen door. 'Heh, Serah, whit's this aboot sangwidges?'

Sarah's voice grew louder as she edged her husband back into the midst of his family, saying, 'You can help me to carry these plates.'

'The only thing Ah'm cairryin' is ma ain breid-basket—tae pit ham an' egg in it!'

Matt, in obvious embarrassment, demanded to know what had gone wrong, and in equal discomfort Maisie explained how it had been decided by the House Committee that it would be an insult to offer Ella anything so plebeian as ham and egg from a kitchen table. At which Ella stepped forward and said:

'But Matt promised me! He said it was a ceremony. I was looking forward to it.'

It was so winsomely done that all Sarah could say was 'Well . . .' and Maisie, realising that the battle had been won, squeezed past the throng and snatched at the more pendulous garments on the pulleys above. As for Sarah, she caught such a look of affection and pride pass from Matt to his fiancée that she knew there was little use making pretences that she could not keep up ——nor would Ella have liked her to. In triumph the patriarch, singing at the top of his voice 'Fall in and follow me,' led his family into the kitchen. They were all thoroughly at home with one another.

CHAPTER 6

WEDDING DAY

SARAH McFLANNEL lay in bed trying not to hear the rhythmic breathing of her husband who, unappalled by the entry into the family circle of one so obviously alien to their working-class traditions, slept the sleep of the just. While she would have resented any hint from Mrs M'Cotton that the McFlannels were of less account than the McSatins, she was aware of a deep uneasiness that, in some way or other, events would prove the folly of Matt's choice. Or would it be of Ella's choice ? Deciding, after hours of tossing, that by the time Matt came home from his next voyage one or other of them might have seen the matter in a different light, she went to sleep. The next night, however, she lay tossing once again for Matt had announced before going to bed, in that self-conscious way he did not seem able to shake off for all his seaworthiness, that he and Ella had decided to get married as soon as he got home on his next leave. Really, thought Sarah, with a lack of originality, young people nowadays just go their own way ! Which indeed Matt and Ella did, so that two evenings before the date fixed for the wedding, Sarah sat in state in the sitting-room opposite her husband waiting for the bride-to-be to appear and make last-minute arrangements. When the door-bell rang, Willie was prodded awake by his wife saying :

' That'll be Ella now. Put on your slippers and button up your vest ! '

Without waiting to make sure that her instructions were being carried out, Sarah went to the door and was for ushering the visitor into a bedroom, but the girl explained pantingly that she had no time for luxuries.

'Come on into the sitting-room then.' Hoping for a measure of presentability on the part of her husband, the woman pushed open the door and said, 'Willie—here's Ella!'

The man came forward genially enough with a kindly 'Hoo' ye?' but instead of shaking hands Ella poked a waggish finger at him.

'Ha, caught you!' she said. 'They made you button up your vest before I came in!'

Sure enough, the buttons and holes did not correspond, but the man was less disconcerted by the circumstance than his wife.

'Ay,' he remarked as he put the matter right, 'they've an awfu job keepin' me up tae scratch. An' the best o't is, if Ah *dae* scratch masel'——'

'Willie, don't be vulgar,' exclaimed Sarah, who never missed a cue-line.

At that, Maisie the bridesmaid came into the room and wanted to know if the bride were jittery. The statement in reply—to the effect that it wanted but thirty-nine hours till the wedding—conveyed the impression that there was an element of nervousness about the leading lady, especially when she added that she had thirty-nine days' work to do! Whereupon Maisie offered to help.

'But you can't,' moaned the bride. 'You can't write letters of thanks for presents. I've got to do it myself. I missed replying to yesterday's lot, and today I got fifteen more.' With a gesture of frustration she turned to her future mother-in-law. 'Imagine! Mrs McFlannel, I've got another standard lamp—that makes three. And two more lemonade sets—that's seven altogether.'

When the commiserations were over, Ella admitted that she had got one really sensible present—a leather pochette with compartments for ration books and clothing coupons.

'Oh!' gasped Sarah. 'The minister!'

The irrelevance was so pronounced that the only one who could find speech was her husband, who said, 'Help ma boab, whit's bitin' ye noo?'

'The minister!' reiterated Sarah. 'I forgot.'

' What on earth,' queried Maisie, ' has the minister got to do with Ella's pochette ? '

' Well, the pochette reminded me of the leather thingummy-jig the Woman's Guild gave to the new minister, and that reminded me, at the church on Sunday he announced from the pulpit he'd be visiting in our street on Thursday night.'

' An' he'll be here the night ! ' exclaimed Willie. ' Jeengs, it's a good thing ye noticed ma vest wisnae buttoned right, Ella.'

At that Maisie looked rather blank and said something about the awkwardness of the situation.

' How can it be awkward ? ' demanded Sarah, who appeared to have recovered her poise. ' I'm glad we're all so comfort-able in the sitting-room instead of in the kitchen. I'll need to look out the Family Bible.'

' But, Mother,' insisted Maisie, ' don't you see—we've rather by-passed him with the wedding arrangements, so——'

' Ach ay,' said Willie, who had reasons of his own for siding with the arrangements referred to, ' but gettin' mairrit by the Sheriff's sichna lot less bother.'

Ella, for her part, had a word in her own defence : ' Matt and I want it that way, Maisie. At least, Matt wanted a church wedding at first, but when he saw how I felt about it he gave in.'

' Well,' said Maisie, ' if the minister comes, you and I had better dodge into the kitchen,' a suggestion which met with no approval from her mother, who insisted that she wanted the minister to meet Ella ; and no-one was under any misapprehen-sion as to the reason for this desire, namely to acquaint the new clergyman with the social standing of the prospective daughter-in-law.

' But don't you see, Mother,' Maisie was being persistent, ' he's sure to wonder why we didn't ask him to tie the knot ? '

Willie rushed to the aid of the bride. ' A' the same, Maisie, if we'd been gettin' a meenister tae tie the knot, it widda been Ella's meenister, wid it no' ? '

' But I haven't got one ! ' Ella's charm lay in her frankness. ' Dad and I have managed to get along quite nicely without the church since we came to live in Glasgow, so getting married by the Sheriff is just the answer to this maiden's prayer.'

Sarah was horror-struck by the confession of such paganism in one she could not help loving, but there was an element of paganism in her own reply as she blurted out, ' I must say, Ella, I'd 've loved to see you in white—coming up the aisle on your father's arm——'

' Ay,' jeered her husband, ' an' a' the weemin greetin' intae their white gloves ! '

Ella turned to her bridesmaid : ' How do *you* feel about it, Maisie ? '

For all her professional front of cynicism Maisie had her own thoughts of romance, which as yet she was unwilling to admit even to herself. She tried to be evasive but failed.

' I don't know,' she blurted out at length ; ' I think I'd feel it was more sort of solemn and binding in a church.'

Willie, once again for reasons of his own, gaped : ' Well, ye better look oot fur somebody else's faither's airm tae hing on tae—Ah'm no' cut oot fur that sorta thing.'

' Don't worry, Dad,' it was Maisie's turn to have recovered her poise ; ' as Peter says, I'm one of nature's spinsters ! '

At that moment the door-bell rang, and Sarah, true to form, teetered : ' Oh dear-dear, that'll be the minister   What would you like to do, Ella ? '

' I rather think I'd like to meet him,' was the smiling reply.

In relief Sarah hustled away, while her husband nudged Ella to ask for a sartorial inspection, but she was too much interested in what Maisie had to say in reply to her question about what the minister was like. ' Has he got a boneless handshake and a holy whine ? ' she added.

' I've never shaken hands with him so I can't tell ! ' Maisie was convinced that she was speaking quite calmly, so she went on : ' His voice is ordinary enough. And I've heard it said he goes in more for conversation than monologues when he's visiting.'

Willie, who could not be expected to know just how grateful his daughter was for his intervention, nudged Ella once more :

' Here—hoo'm Ah noo ?   Is ma vest right ? '

Before Ella had had time to reply, Maisie seized the chance of speaking on a subject upon which she had no embarrassment :

' You're fine, Dad, but it's a pity about your concertina socks,' adding, as the man bent to remove the stigma, ' no—no, you can't pull them up in front of Ella ! '

At that Sarah came back into the room, saying, ' Come away, Mr M'Crepe. I don't think you've actually met our daughter —Maisie ? '

Determined that her secret must be hid more skilfully from this man than from anyone else Maisie adopted a more unsmiling attitude than usual, while the man, not yet knowing what was in his own heart, shook hands with this strange girl and said, just as though she were the plainest of parishioners, ' How d'you do ? ' For all her mother's intuition and capacity for worrying, Sarah was equally unaware of the significance of the introduction, for she turned from it and explained that the other girl was Miss McSatin, who was engaged to Matt. Ella and the young man shook hands while Maisie tried not to be too interested in his back view. As for Willie, he hailed the clergyman affably but informally, having already made his acquaintance at the church.

For a moment or two there was awkwardness while the party got seated. Then, her duties as a hostess weighing heavily upon her, Sarah said :

' You'll be feeling tired, Mr M'Crepe, with climbing all the stairs you've got to in your visiting.'

' Oh, it's not too bad,' said the young fellow in the voice that Maisie had called ordinary, thereby lying in her lovely throat, for she sat there on the edge of the sofa steeling herself against its music. ' When I came to this charge at first, though, I felt I should have served my apprenticeship as a stair-gas-putter-out-er, as Jack Warner would have it.'

Ella bent forward with a smile. ' Do ministers actually listen to the wireless ? ' she asked.

' Of course ! ' was the amazed retort, while Willie demanded to know what good the putting out of stair lights would have been.

' Well, I could have been exercising the necessary leg muscles.'

' Ay,' went on the host, to his daughter's secret delight, ' Glasgow wid be a big chynge fur ye efter workin' in a wee country church.'

' Oh, but I served my time in a shipyard before studying for the ministry,' was the reply, which gave so much pleasure that Willie had to restrain himself from shaking hands albeit belatedly.

' Guid fur you !' he exclaimed instead. ' Ah like a meenister that kens somethin' aboot life—no jist goin' straight f'ae college intae a pulpit. Whit yaird did ye work in ?'

To Sarah this was the signal that the conversation was likely to be protracted ; accordingly she intimated that Maisie would go and put the kettle on.

' Oh, not for me, please !' put in the visitor. ' I've already had to drink five cups of tea since six o'clock so as not to give offence to old ladies.'

' Don't they ever make it coffee ?' asked Ella.

' I'm afraid they don't.'

Willie, whose sense of food was acute, caused a fluttering amongst his female companions by remarking that ministers must get some good feeds at weddings.

' Oh,' spluttered Sarah without any attempt at finesse, ' Mr M'Crepe, how's your mother keeping ?'

' She's very well, thank you, and very glad to be back in her native Glasgow.'

Willie, however, was not to be side-tracked so easily. ' Speakin' aboot weddin' feeds,' he began, ' we're haein' a weddin'——'

This time Maisie plunged into the breach : ' I say, Mother, Peter *is* late tonight, isn't he !'

' So he is,' replied Sarah with gratitude and a little too much emphasis of the fact ; ' I hope nothing's wrong.'

' I don't think I've met Peter,' said the minister obligingly. ' He's the youngest—isn't he ?'

' Fancy you remembering that, Mr M'Crepe !' beamed the mother.

' Well, I'm afraid—if I must be honest, Mrs McFlannel—

68

I've got to confess that your last minister kept a very careful account of the family history of the whole congregation—and I've fallen heir to his notes. Peter's interested in radio engineering, I see.'

And while Maisie looked out of the window her father nipped in with a statement meant to contradict any that might be forthcoming from Sarah about wireless announcers.

Just at that moment there was a bang of the outer door which indicated that Peter had arrived home. Underlining the fact, Willie went on to say that the lad was to be best man at the wedding. This time it was Ella who trailed the red herring by asking where Mr M'Crepe's last charge was, but before he could answer the sitting-room door was flung open and Peter breezed in demanding to know why the family were foregathering there, adding, when he saw the minister and Ella there too, ' Don't tell me it's going to be a church wedding after all ! '

There was a deathly hush while Peter's brick went dropping down into the chasm of discomfort ; then with wonderful aplomb he turned to Ella, saying :

' How's the rushing bride ?   How many hours is it now ? '

' Thirty-eight and three-quarters, Peter. You won't forget the ring, will you ? '   Ella appeared to be tired of the cat-and-mouse game.

' No, *nor* the bridegroom ! ' retorted Peter, unaware of any game ; ' I'll have him on the Sheriff's doormat on the dot.'

To remove from the mind of the minister any lurking doubt Willie came clean with : ' Matt an' Ella are gettin' mairrit by the Sheriff, Mr M'Crepe.'

Sarah gave a wretched little cough, while Maisie tried to hide behind a vase of flowers.

' I'm afraid you've made a mistake, have you not ? ' was Mr M'Crepe's comment.

Ella said, ' Well, you see, I've never had any connection with the Church of Scotland, and it seemed rather insincere to use it for a sort of stage show.'

' Oh, I'm not questioning your sincerity, Miss McSatin,' the young man assured her with a smile which Maisie saw through a haze of petals. ' It's just that—well, were you really under the impression that you could be married by the Sheriff ? '

' Yes. You see, Matt's in the Navy and his ship doesn't get in till tomorrow night, and if it should happen to be an hour or two late we thought there would be less trouble just to walk up to the Sheriff than——'

In self-justification Sarah interjected that it wasn't what she wanted—she wanted it in the church.

' Quite so, Mrs McFlannel,' said the minister soothingly. ' But what I'm trying to point out is that there's no such thing nowadays as getting married by the Sheriff. Actually there never was such a thing, but that was the popular way of describing a marriage not solemnised in church. I'm ever so sorry, but I'm afraid you're going to find things rather awkward.'

' Oh, dear-dear,' wailed Sarah. ' This is terrible—at the last minute too ! ' She was saved from openly accusing her husband of having caused all the trouble by Ella's asking :

' How do you mean " awkward," Mr M'Crepe ? '

' Well, did you say you were expecting to be married on Saturday ? '

' Yes, we understood all we had to do was to appear before the Sheriff with two witnesses to swear that I'd been resident in Scotland for twenty-one days and he'd give us some document to take to the Registrar.'

' Yes—that used to be the procedure, but it's changed now. Of course . . .' He paused, and his audience, for differing reasons, hung on his words, ' Matt's being in the Navy might simplify matters.'

Drowning his mother's ' Oh, isn't this awful ! ' Peter asked how matters were simplified in that way.

' You could apply to the Sheriff for a licence, explaining the circumstances, and if he grants it you'd take it to the minister of the parish in which Miss McSatin resides, and he could nail the banns to the church door, since you want the ceremony performed before Sunday.'

' Oh what a carry on ! ' wailed the affronted mother.

'So I can't do without the church after all?' asked Ella as though she did not want to do without it.

'It rather looks as if you can't!' The young clergyman gave back twinkle for twinkle.

'What a bunch of mutts we've been!' exclaimed Peter. 'And what happens after the banns have been nailed up? Do we all just go to the Registrar and carry on as before?'

'Well, the trouble is——' There was, for the first time, an air of discomfort in the minister's manner.

But Ella was no longer interested in dodging the church. 'Wait a minute!' she interjected. 'Mr M'Crepe—if I can't do without the church, I'm going the whole hog. Can *you* marry me?'

There was a gasp of relief from Sarah as the minister said the matter depended on whether or not the bride lived in his parish.

'My home's just two streets away—in Sandringham Crescent.'

'That's well inside my parish. I'll be very glad to help.'

'Then,' declared Ella, 'Matt's going to get the surprise of his little life—if you can fix it, Mr M'Crepe. Let's blow all the trumpets—"The voice that breathed o'er Eden," and all that sort of thing. Maisie!' she turned to the quiet figure behind her, 'I'll accept that offer of the bridal outfit I told you about. Are you game?'

The quietness of Maisie's assurance was put down by the others as due to excitement, but when she added as circumstantial evidence that she hoped the frock would fit her, Willie was moved to cry out:

'Aw heh, wait! Ah cannae mak' heid nor tail o' a' this. Does this mean Ah've got tae appear noo in ma lum hat an' ma claw-haimmer jaiket?'

'Of course you will!' replied his wife, her tears forgotten. 'O Ella, I'm that glad, you've no idea! It'll seem so much more like a real wedding!'

Ella clapped her future mother-in-law tenderly on the shoulder and addressed the minister once more: 'Mr M'Crepe, if Maisie and I go away now to see to all the details about the

71

frocks and things, will you and Peter fix the rest up between you?'

'Certainly. I'll do all I can to help you.'

'Oh, what a relief!' exclaimed Sarah. 'And we'll tell all our friends to come. Especially Mrs M'Cotton.'

The last three words were mercifully drowned in the confusion of farewells. The occasion seemed to warrant a further confusion of handshaking, and when the two girls found themselves finally outside the door of the sitting-room Ella rubbed her right hand with mock agony.

'I say, Maisie,' she whispered, 'he's got bones in his fingers all right. My hand's sore.'

'So's mine,' said Maisie politely, but she did not think it necessary to add that it was a pleasant kind of soreness.

The next day and a half passed in a whisk of excitement for bride and bridesmaid, but Mrs McFlannel suffered in a froth of her own which bubbled over when Matt's ship was reported as unable to dock before Saturday morning; and when Matt himself finally appeared *via* Ella's home and in no wise upset by the change of plans Sarah was all the more nervy out of sheer perversity. There was an edge to her voice, as zero hour drew near, when she shouted:

'Matt, for goodness' sake hurry up out of that bathroom. You're not the only one that's going to the wedding!'

Exasperatingly Matt's laugh drifted mistily to her as he retorted that there wouldn't be a wedding till he turned up. Then, just to show that she need not confine her worries to one member of the family, her husband waddled up to her, his face wrinkled with self-pity.

'Heh, Serah, thae strippit troosers is ower tight fur me. Look—Ah'll need a bit string tae haud them thegither.'

The harassed woman examined the garment complained of. Right enough, she said to herself, Willie had put on so much weight that she should have realised before now that the matter ought to be attended to.

'Lend him an old pair of your corsets, Mum!' suggested Peter.

'Peter, don't be vulgar, and me so harassed!' She poked at that part of her husband's anatomy which seemed incapable of circumscription. 'Can you not pull in your stomach, Willie?'

'Nae fear! Ah'm wantin' tae leave plenty room fur the big feed we're gettin'.'

'See, turn round till I see if there's anywhere I can let out half an inch.'

'Hauf an inch!' repeated the man in disgust, 'hauf a yaird is mair liker it! Ah'll jist pit on ma auld broon suit.'

'You'll do nothing of the kind. Turn round when you're told.'

While the man was in the act of turning or rather of being turned, Peter asked where his black socks were.

'Oh, Peter, can you not see I'm busy?'

And while Peter was still murmuring about the urgency of his need, Matt appeared on the scene announcing blithely that since he was now finished with the bathroom the rest of the family could have the use of it, and where was the suit he had pressed an hour earlier? Holding on to her restive husband with one hand, with the other Sarah indicated the suit on the kitchen pulley. Peter meanwhile renewed his request for socks.

'Oh, look for them! I laid them out on your dressing-table! Now, Willie, stand still, for goodness' sake!'

Her words were drowned by the screeching of the pulley and Matt's cheerful shout: 'Got the ring all right, Peter?'

'Yes. Would you like me to wear it in my nose so's you'd know it was there?' And off stalked Peter to search once again for his black socks.

'Look out, Dad!' called the sailor. 'Here comes the pulley.'

Willie let out a yell, clutching at his head and altering his stance.

'Sorry, Dad,' said Matt, 'but I told you to look out.'

'Could ye no' a' said "look up"?' Suddenly his groans were turned to yelps. 'Heh, Serah—watch. Ye're kittlin' me!'

Matt drew near to inspect the inspection. 'What's going on here anyway?' he asked, and when the explanation was forthcoming he wanted to know if anybody had a penknife.

' Ay—Ah've got yin in ma workin' jaiket ! ' said the man
with the sore head.

' You mean the jacket that won't work unless you're inside
it ? ' teased Matt with forced gaiety ; ' and not always even then.
Let's see the scissors, Mother.'

' Oh, do be careful, Matt,' jittered Sarah, handing over the
tool required. ' We don't want any accidents and us late as it is.'

' Keep calm, Mother ! What is it Dad says about dying in
the winter ? Look—we'll slit this seam at the back.'

' Oh, you can't do that. What if it was to rip all the way
down in the middle of the church ? '

' Leave it to me, Mother.' The sailor seemed unnaturally
calm and collected. ' Have you a strong linen thread ? I'll
stitch the seam up safe and sound.'

' Ach,' grumbled Willie, ' a' this palaver ! Ah don't see whit
wey ye couldnae 've jist went tae the Manse——'

' Now, Willie ! ' said his wife, ' don't you start that argument
all over again.'

' Heave to, Dad. You're in a bad light. If I jag you I'll
tell you.'

' Ah'll tell *you*, don't be feart ! '

Once more Peter came on the scene with the assurance that
his socks were not to be found, to which Willie, apparently
resigned to his lot, retorted that the lad should wear boots,
thereby obviating the necessity for socks. Sarah left the kitchen
saying, ' Oh, I suppose I better come and get them for you.
Such a fuss over a pair of socks, and there's Maisie getting ready
to be a bridesmaid and never a complaint from her.'

' She's enjoying herself, though,' was the retort.

Meanwhile Willie, excused from the necessity of facing his
son, strove to find the right words of fatherly advice to impart
on the momentous occasion.

' Heh, Matt, Ah widnae 've thocht ye widda hin a steady
enough haun' fur tae dae ony shewin' the day.'

' Oh, I'm taking deep breaths, Dad.' Matt's air of casualness
belied his real feelings.

' Huh—hiv ye a wife in every port ? '

'What do *you* think, Dad?' There was a pause, then he went on, 'Were *you* excited the day *you* were married?'

'Ah cannae mind. Ehm—Matt?'

'Yes, Dad?'

'Ella's a nice lassie.'

'I'm glad you like her. I said you would, remember!' Matt was making an elaborate job of needlework, just as glad of the stage-setting as his father.

'Ah widnae like tae think ye—ye'd hurt 'er feeling's in ony wey.'

Once again there was a pause of embarrassed understanding. 'You're not trying to preach me a sermon, are you, Dad?'

'Naw. Ah hivnae got the richt kinna collar fur that. Ah jist wanted tae tell ye that—that if ye don't mak' a guid man tae that lassie Ah'll—Ah'll set fire tae yer shirt-tail. Noo mind!'

'I'll mind, Dad. But I don't think you need to worry.'

To their mutual relief the door-bell rang and provided a new topic of conversation.

'Help ma boab!' cried Willie, 'that's no' the taxis a'readies. An' me wi' ma shirt tae pit on! Are ye no' near dune yet?'

Matt snipped off the thread. 'There, you'll be as safe as houses. You'll even be able to laugh!'

The kitchen door opened and Sarah came in behind a dazzle of rosebuds and satin ribbon. There was a bouquet for the bridesmaid and one for the bridegroom's mother which could have come from one source only. While the donor was being thanked and scolded on the grounds that he would have to watch every penny from now on as a newly married man, the bridesmaid appeared on the scene belying the assertion made earlier in her favour as to her calmness.

'Mother, Mother!' she clamoured, 'something's gone wrong with this belt. See if it's twisted at the back. Oh, hurry, I'll be late! What's the time?'

Peter poked her playfully. 'Huh, keep your hair on! You were being held up to me a minute ago as a shining example.'

75

'You shut your trap !' she snapped back.

'U-uh—temper !' snapped Peter in turn.

'Now that's not the way to talk to her !' said Sarah.

'Well, she asked for it !'

The atmosphere was becoming too overwrought for Matt, who picked up his suit and left the kitchen. As for the overwrought mother, her brain reeled for the next ten minutes in the mounting excitement of her family's last-moment demands. 'Ah cannae find ma back stud, Serah ! Come on an' help me tae look fur it !' 'Mother, where did you put that velvet pad I had for my hat ?' 'I can't get this shoe-strap to work, Mother. Mother ! Where are you ?' 'Heh, Serah, help me intae this jaiket !' 'Mother, have you change for half a crown ?' 'Quick, Mother, fix this head-dress for me, it's caught in my hair at the back !' 'Serah, look ! Hoo d'ye like me in ma lum hat ? Heh, Serah—if Ah wis a younger man wid ye mairry me again ? Aw, Serah, it widnae take ye a meenit jist tae *look* !' 'Mother, this suitcase is going to be too small. Is there a bigger one ?' 'Has anybody seen the wedding ring ? Mother, what did you do with the wedding ring ? I laid it on the table there !' 'Mother, isn't the taxi late ? What's the time ? Is that clock right ? Look, Mother—how's my skirt at the back ?' 'Mother, Mother, where are you ? Oh, here you are—what's the matter?'

The bridegroom had run his bewildered mother to earth at the door of the lobby press. There was an audible sniff as she replied from the darkness thereof : 'I was looking out another suitcase for you, Matt.'

'Oh, but I got everything into the one I had, after all. Poor wee Mother. You've just been dancing attendance on us all, and nobody's looked after you. See, turn round. Your hat's on crooked. Let me put it straight for you. There. . . .' The adjustment made, Matt peered into the face beneath. 'I say— you haven't been crying, have you ?'

'O Matt !' The sniffs were frank tears now. 'My wee Matt ! You're not going to be my son any more.'

'But that's just nonsense, Mother. You know quite well I'll always be your son.'

'No-no. You know the old saying, "My son's my son till he gets him a wife."'

'Mother, look at me!' He took her by the shoulders.

'O Matt, I can't. You're going away to leave me.'

'But I've been leaving you for the last six years, haven't I?'

'Yes, but that was different! This was your home. Now you'll be going to another house and I won't have any more right to scold you!'

'Come on, you wouldn't like me to desert Ella at the church door, would you, now?'

There was a sigh. 'No—ehm—Matt, you're getting a nice wee wife.'

'I know. It frightens me sometimes when I think how lucky I am.'

'She's a real lady. I don't mean just that she's gentry—it's —well—she's a gem, Matt. You won't ever—do anything that would give her a sore heart, will you, Matt?'

For the second time that day Matt knew his inarticulate parents were trying to give advice that would have been too late had they not, for all his conscious days, already instilled into him by the power of their own example the integrity that had made him what he was.

'I won't give Ella a sore heart, Mother,' was all he could say. 'You know she likes you a lot?'

'Does she? Not any more than I like her. I'm real proud to be getting her for a daughter.' Once again the tears flowed freely and Sarah dabbed ineffectually at her eyes. 'O Matt, if you see me crying in the church—you'll not laugh, will you?'

'I'll not laugh, Mother. Come on—give me what Dad calls a wee cheeper.'

As their lips met the door-bell rang announcing the arrival of the taxis. Sarah snatched at her fleeting opportunities.

'Goodbye, son. I hope you and Ella will be happy.'

77

CHAPTER 7

TEA FOR FIVE

SARAH McFLANNEL sat at her fireside on the following Monday afternoon. An overwhelming lassitude had prevented her from attending to the week's washing, and she stared into the sulky fire, too weary to get up and put on more coal. Besides, she had a disturbing pain in the region of her stomach. She prodded it, wondering if it were appendicitis as a result of something she had eaten at the wedding on Saturday, and visualising the trouble she would cause if she had to go into the infirmary and leave her family to fend for themselves. She had got the length of being glad, for her reputation's sake, that she was still wearing the underwear she had worn on Saturday, when the weariness increased like a thick cloud and she fell fast asleep in her chair. She was still there when, two hours later, her husband and son arrived home from their work. They stood aghast at the kitchen door, the first reaction of the man of the house being that the evening meal was not even set.

'Mother must be out !' exclaimed Peter.

'The fire's oot onywey !' observed Willie. Then he caught sight of the slowly awakening woman in the chair. 'Heh, Serah, whit's up that ye're sittin' doon ?'

'Oh,' she mumbled thickly, 'I haven't been well. Oh dear, the fire's out. Oh, and the tea's not set. Oh !'

Peter was at her side by this time. 'Don't get up, Mum,' he insisted, ' you're not looking very fit. What's the matter ?'

'Ye're the colour o' a dish-cloot,' said Willie. 'Hiv ye been seek ?'

'I had a pain. I'm still—a wee bit confused. I think I must 've fainted. What time is it ?'

78

'It's six o'clock,' her husband told her, then with sudden tenderness he bent over her and asked what was wrong. But Sarah could not tell him and her statement that her head was queer was jumbled up with her query whether Maisie had got home yet.

'She's got a date with a dressmaker tonight, Mum. Don't you remember she's been telling us all week-end about it ?'

But Sarah's memory was as weak as her physical condition as she tried to rise, saying that she would have to get the fire lit. She let out a yelp of pain as she fell back in the chair again.

'Serah, lass !' Willie was genuinely perturbed by this time. 'Is it wind, d'ye think ?'

'Oh, I don 't know,' she moaned, ' my head's so funny.'

'I tell you what, Mum,' said Peter, 'I'll run down to the phone at the corner of the street and get the doctor to come and have a look at you.'

'No-no. I'm not as bad as all that !' She made another attempt to rise. 'Maybe if I had a drink of hot water. . . .'

'Pit on the kettle, Peter !' barked Willie, and as the lad bounced to comply he took his wife's hand in his and said, ' Ye'll need tae get well, hen. Ah don't like tae see ye lookin' sae felled.'

'Tell Peter not to fill the kettle. I only want a sip or two.'

Partly because he was afraid his voice might betray his emotions and partly to make himself heard above the roar of water cascading into the kettle, he bellowed, ' Heh, Peter, it's no' a bath yer mother's needin'.'

Peter called back that he was boiling enough water to do for the tea at the same time.

'Tae hang wi' wur tea. Pour hauf o' that oot !' Willie added more power to his tones.

'Don't shout, Willie,' pleaded the patient. ' It makes my head ding.'

He was immediately contrite. 'Ah'm sorry, lass. Here, Ah tell ye whit, Ah'll open oot the bed-settee an' you can lie doon.'

'Oh, never mind. It clutters up the kitchen so much when the bed's standing out in the middle of the floor. Just leave me alone. I'll be all right. I hope Maisie isn't going to be long.'

'Ach, whit does it maitter if it diz clutter up the place. Wha's carin' whit it looks like if you're no' weel. Ye'd be faur better lyin' doon.'

She gave in, not having the strength to argue the point. So the contraption that was a settee by day was manhandled so that its machinery extended six feet into the middle of the floor and the nocturnal character of its capabilities was revealed. Between them father and son got the woman's slippers off and her unwilling body persuaded to lie prone on top of the bed-clothes with a down quilt over her. Slowly her worries returned and found expression.

'It seems terrible me not having your tea ready.'

'Don't you worry,' her husband assured her. 'Ah'm no' wantin' ony tea if you're no' weel.'

'The worst of it is, I was going out for fish and some cakes this afternoon, but I didn't manage. But there's a tin of corned beef you could open.'

The unhungry man said, 'Nae bully beef for me. Ony ham?'

Sarah swallowed quickly and said it had all been eaten on Sunday. Seeing the gulp, Peter suggested that the topic of food might be abandoned.

'Oh, I wish Maisie was here,' sighed Sarah, adding, one worry ahead of the others, 'I don't want to be a burden to you.'

'Come on, Mum,' said Peter, 'it's not like you to talk like that. You've likely eaten something that hasn't agreed with you; greasy kippers or something.'

'Heh—wha's talkin' aboot food noo?' The complaint came from his father. 'She's maybe jist needin' a dose o' ile.'

Sorry for herself, Sarah pointed out that it wasn't fair that they should belittle her illness.

'There-there, lass. We're only tryin' fur tae cheer ye up. Ye'll need tae hurry up an' get well, ye ken. Ah need ye tae look efter me.'

Peter, at the other side of the bed, tucked the quilt with unnecessary firmness about his mother as he said, 'Now you're not to pay the slightest attention to Dad and me. Try and get a wee sleep if you can. We'll likely make an awful muddle of things, but as long as you don't see it, it doesn't matter.'

'Thanks, Peter. I'm really feeling a bit better already. Just awful sleepy.'

'That's the stuff!' Peter stroked the hair from her forehead with a tenderness she had not believed possible in him. 'Dad and I will try to keep quiet.'

Sarah closed her eyes contentedly, murmuring, 'Never mind the hot water now.'

Peter tiptoed round to where his father still stood gaping helplessly, took him firmly by the arm and led him to the scullery where he whispered, 'I'll light the fire if you make the tea ready.'

'But Ah don't ken whit's fur the tea!' said Willie, not whispering. 'Dae you?'

'No, but we're not going to waken her up to ask her.'

'There's dried egg,' came the sleepy remark from the bed.

'Whit's that?' asked Willie.

'I said,' more clearly, 'there's dried egg.'

'Whaur?'

'Oh, Dad,' said Peter, 'let's look for it ourselves and not bother Mother.'

'But Ah don't ken whit tae dae wi' dried egg!'

'There'll be instructions on the packet!' the fierce whisper came from Peter.

'Whit aboot you daein' the cookin', well?'

'No fear! I know my own limitations.'

'Ach, whit wey had Maisie tae go an' see a dressmaker the night—o' a' nights!'

'Oh, Dad, surely the two of us can guddle along for one meal. The egg stuff'll be in the press there.'

'Whit press?'

'The one before your nose! See, I'm going to light the fire. I think you should set the tea-table before you start. The egg won't take long to cook.'

'Ach!' the man's disgust knew no bounds—'whaur's the tablecloth?'

'Search me!'

Willie lifted up his voice, ' Serah, whaur's——'

' Shsh, Dad ! Don't bother Mother ! '

' Ach you ! We'll no' bother wi' a tablecloth.'

Scrabbling about in the coal-bunker Peter pointed out that the polished top of the table might suffer through lack of a tablecloth.

' We'll pit doon a newspaper, well. Seein' there's jist you an' me sittin' doon.'

' Okay. Here's hoping Mother doesn't waken up.'

With elaborate care Willie spread his evening newspaper on the table. When Peter had got the fire going and had leisure in which to admire his father's efforts, he discovered that the butter-dish had been dispensed with, and that instead the week's ration, still in its paper wrapping, was tastefully decorating the centre of the table, flanked on the one side by a pot of jam which had been broached by rule of thumb, and on the other by the whole loaf of bread. That this latter was an English fashion did not occur to the table-setter who, on being reminded of the absence of saucers from the equipment, said that mugs did not need saucers, adding :

' Neither o' us takes sugar in wur tea, so we don't need teaspoons.'

' I see you're all set for a picnic tea ! '

Willie dusted his hands. ' Ach, there's faur too much falder-allin' when weemin gets their hauns on things. Life wid be faur mair easy if men had the runnin' o' a hoose.'

As though to say ' hear-hear ' the door-bell tinkled twice, causing consternation in the kitchen.

' Help ma boab,' said Willie, ' Ah bet ye that's the M'Cotton wife.'

' Shsh,' said Peter, forgetting to whisper. ' If we keep quiet maybe they'll go away.'

' Whit if it's ma rich uncle f'ae Australia, but ? '

' Well, away you go to the door.'

' Naw, you go ! '

' I can't ! My hands are black with coal ! '

With a look of annoyance on his face and a grumble in his

throat, Willie, true to his habit of hospitality, went to the door, saying in answer to Peter's S O S, that he would tell the caller to return the following day. When he opened the outside door, however, he found someone standing there he could not refuse to admit. It was the young minister.

'I hope I haven't called at an awkward time, Mr McFlannel,' said the young man, accepting the cordial invitation to step inside, 'but I wanted to see Peter, and I thought I could be surer of getting him now than later in the evening.'

'Ay; he's in the kitchen. We're in a bit o' a habble—the wife's no' weel, but you'll be used wi' seein' folk in bed. Jist go right in.' He stood aside to let Mr M'Crepe pass, yelling at the same time, 'Heh, Peter, here's the meenister tae see ye!'

Peter was suitably shocked but managed to mutter an apology for having been caught on the wrong foot.

'I'm sorry to see Mrs McFlannel's in bed,' said the visitor; 'nothing serious, I hope?'

At that, consciousness returned to the patient. She sat up, gaped about her, at the bed, at her men-folk, at the visitor.

'Oh, Mr M'Crepe!' she exclaimed; then catching sight of the table she shuddered. 'Oh, look at the table. And the minister here! Oh, what a sight!'

'Ach well, Serah, we couldnae be bothered makin' a splash seein' it wis jist Peter and me.'

'Splash!' The woman was almost in tears. 'And to think how nice everything always is! And for Mr M'Crepe to see it like that! Peter—what *were* you thinking about?'

'It wasn't me, Mum. I was lighting the fire!'

'Don't worry, Mrs McFlannel,' interposed Mr M'Crepe, eager to set her at her ease, 'when I'm alone I'm afraid I don't bother much with tablecloths myself.'

But Sarah refused to be comforted. 'It's awful nice of you to say that, Mr M'Crepe, but I don't think you ever sat down to a table like that!'

'Aw cheer up, Serah. Ye never died a winter yet!'

Whereat the sorely tried woman flopped back on to the pillow once more and complained that her head was like to split.

The minister made another attempt at consolation. ' I wonder if I could do anything to help. I've done a lot of camp cooking.'

Like a flash Willie rapped out, ' Can you cook dried egg ? '

From the bed, her hand covering her shamed eyes, Sarah said, ' Willie, you shouldn't talk like that to a minister.'

' There's nothing wrong with the way he's speaking, Mrs McFlannel. We ministers are far more human than folk give us credit for. The only snag is, I don't know anything about cooking dried egg.'

' I tell you what,' said Peter, ' if you'll sit down there and talk to Mother, Mr M'Crepe, Dad and I'll manage ourselves.'

The retort won Sarah's admiration. ' But I really don't think your mother wants to be talked to ! '

Unabashed, Willie suggested that the visitor might care to share the contemplated meal, a proposition that brought Sarah to a sitting posture again.

' Oh, Willie—from that table ! '

A gentle hand pushed her down again, a quiet voice assured her that the speaker would be glad to have a meal. In amazement she heard him address the other two :

' I say, let's put the thing on an orderly duty basis. Mr McFlannel to cook the dried egg, Peter to cut the bread and things, and I'll set the table. I think, for Mrs McFlannel's peace of mind, we'd be better to have a proper tablecloth.'

' That's awful considerate of you,' conceded Sarah, ' but I think it's terrible for the minister to be treated like a house-maid.'

' Don't you worry. I'm enjoying myself. If you could just tell me where to find a tablecloth.'

' In the drawer in the dresser there—there's a clean tea-cloth—a big embroidered one.'

' Right you are ! Now just you close your eyes and try to get to sleep ; everything's under control.'

' I don't think I could sleep for shame, Mr M'Crepe, you seeing the house in this state. I'd rather get up——'

' Now look here, Mrs McFlannel, my father died when I was a kid, and my mother went out to work to eke out her widow's pension. My brother and I were message boys for a spell, and lots of times the house wasn't just in apple-pie order. If you could just relax and let me be one of the family, you'd be doing me a favour.'

Sarah made a brave effort to relax, murmuring something about kindness. She was not so relaxed, however, as to miss hearing the diffident question :

' Is—ehm—Miss Maisie—is she away from home just now ? '

' She's at the dressmaker's tonight or this would never have happened.'

She wondered if he were specially interested, but his next remark chased her dreams before they had taken shape. ' Well, when she comes home she'll find we've got along nicely even although we *are* only men.'

She accepted the feeble joke with a feebler smile.

' Where's the bread knife ? ' asked Peter as though in evidence of male competency.

' In the table-drawer in the scullery. There's only a heel of a loaf in the bread tin, though.'

There was a shout of triumph from the scullery : Willie had found the tin of dried eggs. A bowl wherein to mix the stuff eluded him, however. His query conveyed the impression that the printed instructions on the packet ought to have been more localised.

' You'll get the bowl on the shelf above the cooker,' called the invalid, ' but, Willie, you can't offer the minister dried egg for his tea.'

' Well, we're no' offerin' 'im bully beef ! ' came the reply. ' " Take one level tablespoon dried egg . . ." '

The worried face on the pillow called forth the suggestion from the minister that if he was being a nuisance he would clear out, ' but,' he added, ' I'm enjoying myself, honestly ! '

' I wouldn't like your suit to get messed up,' Sarah protested. ' Oh, it seems terrible me lying here and the minister doing my work for me.'

' Look, I'll take off my jacket if that'll ease your mind any.' And off came the jacket.

Willie, pausing in his search for a spoon, gaped at the spectacle. 'Jeengs, Ah've never seen a meenister in 'is shirt sleeves afore !'

Peter giggled. 'Yes—and look, Dad—he's like me—he turns up his sleeves when his cuffs are dirty !'

Properly scandalised, Sarah said, 'Peter, what a way to talk !' but nobody heeded her, for Willie was saying :

'Here, Ah've aye wondered—that black dickie thing—hoo's it held doon ?'

'Willie ! Don't be irreverent !'

'That's no' irreverent—it's jist plain curiosity ! Ah used tae think it wis a black shurt youse meenisters wore.'

The male model was obliging. 'No, look,' he said, 'it's fastened here.' He indicated the place. 'And it's called a stock, not a dickie.'

'My, it's a queer-like contraption !' observed Willie with candour. 'But it must save ye somethin' on ties. Can ye wear yer collar the right way roon when ye're on holiday ?'

'Oh, Willie !'

'Ah hear ye, Serah !' was the irrepressible retort. 'Jist you lie doon, hen. Ye're getting' gey rid in the face. Ah'll away an' see aboot that dried-egg stuff !' And he trotted back to the scullery mumbling his formula about one level tablespoon.

Suiting the action to his words, Mr M'Crepe said that he would put what was already on the table on to the dresser so as to get the cloth spread, adding, 'You know, Mrs McFlannel, you ought to feel flattered that it takes three men to do the job of one woman !'

Said Peter, 'I think Mother's feeling more flattened than flattered.'

'I hope not !' replied the tablemaid. 'I say, Peter, I really came up tonight to ask a favour of you.'

But Peter was not greatly interested. 'Ugh !' he grumbled, 'I'm making a right muck of this loaf I'm trying to slice.'

'If you turned it on its side it would be easier !'

When the new method had been successfully adopted the minister renewed the attack : 'I was wondering if you could give me a hand with my Youth Club that I'm hoping to start next winter.'

'Me?' gasped the lad, 'but I've never done—I mean —I'm not that kind of chap. I mean to say. . . .'

Ignoring the stumbling protests Mr M'Crepe went on: 'I had the notion—you'll tell me if it's practicable—to have the young chaps doing some manual work one night in the week —say building a wireless set from scratch—and I don't mean anything to do with cat's whiskers. . . .' Peter sniggered politely. 'And I wondered if—since you're a radio electrician —you could perhaps give advice?'

'Well,' answered the embarrassed Peter, 'actually it's not that kind of radio I've specialised in, but I think the scheme's a sound one. I'm a great believer in giving young folks something to do,' he added from the depths of his own callow experience. 'Keep 'em off the streets!'

'Well, supposing you were to come along some night?'

While Peter hesitated, his father could be heard memorising the immortal words: 'Put the dried egg into a clean bowl, add the water and mix till smooth.'

'I'll think about it,' the young fellow said at length.

'Will it take much thinking?'

Peter replied with another question: 'What night had you intended?'

'Wednesdays.' Betraying no self-consciousness that Sarah could detect, the minister went on: 'I say, should I put down a cup and saucer for Miss Maisie?'

'Oh, she'll not be here for ages yet!' answered Peter. 'I'm afraid the Youth Club's no-go as far as I'm concerned. Wednesday's my psychology night.'

'Are you studying psychology?'

'Well, in a mild kind of way.'

'Then you're just the chap I'm looking for!' For a moment or two the conversation lapsed as Peter thought out a new excuse. Willie's murmurings filtered through:

' "Work out the lumps with a spoon against the side of the bowl." ' When he came once again to the kitchen to search for the appropriate spoon, Mr M'Crepe took the chance to ask if a doctor had been called for Mrs McFlannel. Peter replied that the idea had been rejected by the patient herself, while Willie moved around noisily, quoting further extracts from his Book of Words.

'Ah've tae whip slightly wi' a fork or a whisk,' he grumbled. 'Whitna palaver fur a spunefu' o' poother!' He fingered the cutlery lying in a cluster at the end of the table. 'Which o' thur's a whisk?' he demanded.

'Shsh, Dad! Mother's trying to sleep!' Peter conducted his father back to the scullery. 'Look—there's the whisk hanging up on that nail at the edge of the shelf!'

Willie indicated that the article was hiding there from malice aforethought and hauled it down roughly.

'About this Youth Club, Peter,' persisted Mr M'Crepe.

'Yes?' Peter did not sound over-enthusiastic.

'D'you think—um—is there any chance that—um—your sister might be interested?'

Sarah's eyes opened; a close observer might have failed to observe any evidences of headache.

'I'm sure I don't know. You could always ask her.'

'I mean to!' was the frank response.

At that Willie came on the scene carrying the bowl. 'Ah cannae get thae knots oot!' he complained.

'Knots?' asked Peter with wilful stupidity. 'Where does the string come in, Dad?'

'The knots in this egg stuff!'

'Oh, lumps?' Now that the attack seemed to have veered in his sister's direction, Peter could afford to be jocular. 'You likes it or you lumps it, eh, Dad?'

Willie turned on his heel. 'Ah'll jist bung the hale dollop intae the pan. The heat'll maybe take the lumps oot!'

'I say, Peter,' said the table-setter suddenly, 'I think I hear your sister coming in. Hand me over my jacket!'

But before it could be reached the door was flung open and the sight that greeted the girl's eyes made her gasp out:

'What's this in aid of?'

88

'Oh, Maisie,' exclaimed her mother, sitting up, 'they won't let me get up. I was sick this afternoon.'

'Poor wee Mother ! Have you a pain ?'

'No, I'm a lot better. I think I could get up now. Oh, Maisie, I feel so ashamed that Mr M'Crepe should see the place like this !'

Something of that shame was even now spreading itself irritatingly over Maisie's face as she acknowledged the greeting from the visitor ; it found its way into her voice, which seemed to acquire a new edge to it as she exclaimed :

'No wonder you're ashamed, Mother ! I never saw the table looking like that ! The tablecloth's on the wrong side up for one thing. Peter, you mutt, could you not have seen the knots in the embroidery were facing the wrong way ?' She ignored her brother's protests as she carried on : 'And would you look at the cups and saucers ! All standing round the table at everybody's place ! I'm sure you've seen the way Mother does it hundreds of times ! You *are* a dope !'

As Peter burst out laughing the real villain of the piece went into the witness-box, confessing that he had been table-setting orderly.

'Oh ? Then it's me that's the dope !' Maisie joined in her brother's laughter. 'I'm terribly sorry, Mr M'Crepe. I say, where's Dad ?'

'He's doing an all-in wrestling match with some dried egg in the scullery !' Peter told her.

'Oh, Maisie !' called her mother, 'will you see what he's up to ? You never know. . . .'

She went into the scullery calling, 'Hullo, Dad. What's cookin', good lookin' ?'

'Oh, ye're there, Maisie. Well, ye're too late. Ah've made scrambled egg. Smell !'

Maisie smelt. 'The stink's quite like the thing, but it looks like something the cat had brought up. I'll see to it.'

'Away you go an' lea'e me alane. Ah'm fine. It's thae young fellas in there that's needin' help. This'll be ready in a brace o' shakes o' a bumbee's ankle.'

But Maisie refused to budge. She peered into the pot again. 'Dad, did you expect to feed the lot of us from that small mess of pottage?'

'Is there no' enough there?' asked the cook in amazement. 'Ach well, youse can hiv the bully beef yer mother's been talkin' aboot. Ah'll eat this masel'.'

There was a feeble call from the kitchen, and Maisie rushed to answer.

'Maisie,' cried Sarah, 'go into the sitting-room and get a tin of tongue that's at the back of the right-hand drawer in the sideboard. You'll get a tin of peaches there too, and a tin of cream. I was hiding them from your father.'

The young people exchanged looks of amusement at this statement, but Sarah had ceased to mind what they thought of her.

'And in the press—on the top shelf—I've got a piece of sultana cake behind a row of books, and there's some chocolate biscuits in the jelly-pan on the top shelf of the scullery.'

'You're a great wee dodger, Mother,' said Maisie as she left the kitchen.

'Peter, if you'll take Mr M'Crepe into the sitting-room for a wee while, I'll get up.'

'You'll stay where you are!' was Peter's retort. 'We're all set to make a fuss of you. Dad's promised to make some of his famous toast for you.'

Sarah lay back, saying, 'Oh—toast! That would be nice. It's the one and only thing he can make. Of course it's easy for him—he just lets everything else go by the board while he stands and watches his precious toast.'

At that the minister came forward, fully clothed and apparently in his right mind, saying that he had found not only the tray but also the tray-cloth, which he was prepared to swear was right-side-up. The woman basked in the unaccustomed care, assuring them she was feeling very much better. She lay with her eyes closed, allowing the murmur of voices and the jingle of preparations to flow past her, dreaming dreams that would have horrified her daughter even then coming back into the kitchen, her arms laden.

'Well, folks, here we are. One piece of sultana cake. One tin of peaches. One tin of cream. And one tin of tongue.'

As the articles were severally dumped on the table the cook came from the scullery, the toasting-pan in his hand. He gaped.

'Whit's that? Tongue? No' bully beef efter a'! Here, whaur's the dug?'

He hurried back to the scullery and emerged this time with the 'mess of pottage.' He whistled.

'Heh, Susan! Come 'ere an' eat this dried egg!'

CHAPTER 8

RADIO-ACTIVITY

I

WHEN the meal was over and a promise had been extracted from Peter to help with the Youth Club, and even Maisie had shown a non-committal interest in it, the young minister went away, and although she tried to read into his good-night wishes something special for her daughter, Sarah had to admit in the cold light of the following morning that there was nothing to go on. For a day or two she toyed with the idea of inviting the minister's mother to the house some afternoon, but finally abandoned it in favour of the principle of letting things take their course.

For the next few weeks life seemed uneventful enough. Matt was on a short voyage, and when he came home it would not be to his father's house but to the exotic flat in Sandringham Crescent which Ella shared with her father and brother. Sighing, Sarah hoped that this arrangement would work all right, but she had her fears.

As for Maisie, she too had her fears. She was afraid to allow her thoughts to wander too much in a certain direction, and to that end she went regularly to church, excusing this paradoxical course of action under the plea that she would be better to see how many other girls were casting furtive glances at the young minister as he mounted the pulpit, his red hood enhancing his fresh complexion and black hair. She was a fool, she told herself.

Peter was suffering acutely from delayed adolescence. He had steered a safe course through the ' properly organised state of society ' wilderness, he was no longer interested in girls (he felt sure), and was now devoted to his work through the day and to his elementary psychology in those evenings on which the Workers' Educational Association provided that branch of adult education. On Saturday afternoons he went cycling, and on one of his trips he found himself in the Milngavie outskirts being hailed by an elderly woman.

' Hullo, Peter ! Oot fur a run on yer bike ? '

' Hullo, Mrs McTweed ! What are you doing out here— have you taken up hiking ? '

' Me ? Naw—Ah'm goin' hame. Ah'm sayin' Ah'm goin' hame ! '

He resisted the tendency to smile at the repetitive style of speech. ' Aren't you living in the town now ? '

' Naw—Ah flittit jist last week tae a wee cottage oot the road here.'

' Are you staying all alone ? '

' That's right. Ah'm sayin' that's right ! '

' Some change from a Glasgow tenement, eh ? '

' Ach, Ah got that fed up wi' folk livin' above me that Ah made up ma mind Ah wis gonnae try fur a bungalow.'

' And have you got one ? '

' Well, it's no' jist whit ye wid ca' a bungalow like thon wumman M'Cotton's—it's jist a wee but an' ben, but ach, it diz me fine. Ah'm sayin' it diz me fine ! '

' Are you not lonely ? '

' Me lonely ? Naw—no' yet onywey. It's a sichna relief no' tae hae weans stampin' an' stumpin' ower ma heid. Manys a time when ma man wis alive an' tryin' fur tae get tae sleep through the day wi' him bein' a baker, Ah coulda throttled thae weans ! '

' I'm sure ! ' giggled Peter. ' Including the wee McFlannels ! '

' Ay,' she acknowledged with candour, ' but bad an' a' as youse yins wis, ye couldnae haud a caunle tae this last lot.'

' Don't you find it a long road to carry your messages ? '

' Ach, there's aye the vans. Ah'm sayin' there's aye the vans—bakers an' grocers an' theym. Ah'm gettin' on fine. There's jist one thing, but ! '

93

'Oh! What's that?'

'Ma wireless. It's no' goin' right. Ye'd think they were aye fryin' sausages at the BBC, an' every noo an' again it squeals like blue murder.'

'Oh, that would be a soprano taking a top note.'

'Huh.' She dismissed his pleasantry with contempt. 'An' then whiles it dies away till Ah can hardly hear it—the folk at the ither end seem tae be whusperin' like as if there wis a deid corp' in the next room.'

'You've been tuned in to the Third Programme, Mrs McTweed! I'll need to have a look at your set.'

'Will ye? That's real decent o' ye, Peter. Could ye manage it the day?'

Peter looked so uncomfortable at this fast method of work that the woman had the grace to apologise. He mumbled something about meeting another chap at Blanefield.

'Oh well, here, don't let me keep ye. Jist you jump on yer bike. Ah wish Ah wis young enough tae get comin' on yer back step.'

Peter was preparing to mount again when she went on :

'Oh, here—d'ye ever see thon niece o' mine, Ivy?'

The affair between him and Ivy McTweed was now so far in the past that he could speak without discomfort about it as he assured her blithely that he had not seen the girl for ages.

'Ye were weel rid o' hur!' exclaimed the aunt. 'Ah'm sayin' ye were weel rid o' hur. She's a nasty bit o' work, thon. No' one o' that tribe did a haun's turn fur me when Ah wis flittin'; but wait an' you'll see—they'll be comin' oot in their thoosan's when they fin' oot Ah've got a wee cottage in the country. But ach, away ye go an' no' let me taigle ye. Ah'm sayin'——'

'I tell you what,' Peter broke into the reiteration, 'how would it do if I came out next Saturday afternoon—I could have a squint at your set and put up an aerial—I don't suppose you've got one just now?'

'Naw, Ah hivnae. Right ye are, then, Ah'm sayin' right

ye are. An' ye can stey fur yer tea although ye'll no' get much, Ah'm feart. One ration book disnae——'

'Don't you worry about me,' he called back from a distance of fifty yards, 'I'll be seeing you !'

2

When he had not returned from his cycle run in time for tea, his mother was inventing colourful reasons for his absence. When Maisie told her not to worry, Willie piped up : 'Yer mother could nae mair help worryin' than she can help ripin' ma pooches when Ah'm sleepin.'

'Willie,' exclaimed the indignant woman, 'I do *not* ripe your pooch—pockets !'

'Ach well, ye'd be better tae resign yersel' tae the fact that Peter's been run ower by a bus an' be done wi't. If we were a' in wur graves ye wid be able tae stop worryin' !'

'It's not fair of you to make a fool of me like that. And anyway, you're always reading about accidents to bikes.'

'Ach, cheer up. Ye never died a winter yet !'

'Oh, will you *never* stop saying that stupid thing. It doesn't make sense.'

'Does it no' ? Ach well, cheer up onywey. Here's Peter.'

Unaware of the stir he had caused in his mother's nervous system, Peter came in demanding to know if his tea was ready.

'Ready ?' she snapped. 'Will you look at the time—tea was ready hours ago !'

The lad refused to be impressed. 'We must've gone farther than we thought. I'm starving—I could eat a scabby horse.'

'U-uh, Peter !' warned Maisie, 'you know how Mother feels about vulgarity.'

'That's not vulgarity—it's horse sense !' he retorted with a hoot at his own wit. Turning to his mother who was setting before him the remains of macaroni-and-cheese in a state of perfect preservation, he went on, 'I met an old pal of yours this afternoon—Mrs McTweed !'

Sarah was interested, especially when he went on to explain about her living in a wee cottage 'at the back of beyond.'

'Good grief!' exclaimed Maisie, 'what'll she do now without people to complain about for their ham-ham-hammerin'? Ah'm sayin', their ham-ham . . .'

For Peter the reiteration had gone beyond a joke. He gulped down his food with the statement that he understood the lady had gone there to be rid of the noise.

'She must be awful lonely out there,' was Sarah's opinion.

'She's got the wireless.' In the pause made by the passage of macaroni, Maisie took the chance to remark, 'My sainted aunt!' but in a moment Peter went on, 'It's not going very well though, so I've promised to have a look at it—next Saturday afternoon.' After another pause as before-mentioned, he mumbled, 'I say, Mum——'

'I'm sorry, that's all that was left in the pie-dish.'

'It's not that. I was wondering—how would it do if we all went out to see her? I mean—she's bound to miss her husband and all that.'

'Oh, but,' protested the housewife, 'we couldn't all land ourselves on her without warning. What with rationing and all that.'

'Well, why not a picnic? You know—you could make up sandwiches and things—and all she'd need to provide would be the cups and saucers.'

'When did you join the Boy Scouts?' teased Maisie.

Willie was so taken with the idea that he actually offered to assist in the repair of the wireless set.

'Thanks for the offer, Dad,' murmured Peter dubiously.

'Had you thought of anything Mother and I could do while you and Dad are mucking about with the wireless?' There was a hint of a sneer in Maisie's voice.

'Well, you could always help to wash up the dishes.'

'Oh, could we! What a perfect example of masculine imagination! Always jumping to the conclusion that women *like* housework! "In a properly organised state of society——"'

'Get hur a soap box, somebody,' shouted Willie.

'It's my line anyway, Dad!' complained Peter.

A semblance of peace being restored, they got down to an amicable discussion for the outing Peter had arranged for them, so that when Saturday morning dawned bright and clear, even Sarah felt a thrill of anticipation.

3

The bus dropped them at the end of the road leading to Mrs McTweed's cottage, and when the occupant opened her door and saw them all standing there her reiterations knew no bounds.

'Come-in-come-in!' was her culminating remark of welcome.

As she bowed her head going through the low door, Sarah said she was surprised to hear about the change of address; and while the men were looking round for the wireless they had come to mend, Mrs McTweed fussed and bustled with her unexpected visitors, answering Sarah's surprise with reiterated assurances of her own surprise and pleasure. The attaché case full of sandwiches 'and things' was opened, causing further surprise.

'My, that wis awful nice o' ye! Here wis me staunin' at the door there sayin', "Come-in-come-in" an' at the back o' ma mind Ah'm sayin' tae masel', "Oh help, there's jist the heel o' a loaf in the breid box!"'

The men, having examined the interior of the plywood receptacle, decided to erect an aerial, and, having come armed with the requisite wire and other equipment, they assured her that all they now required from her was a pair of kitchen steps. While Peter went to get them from the shed, Willie said he would be better to go and help him, adding that if he spat on his hands often enough he would be given credit for doing some work. As he left the cottage, Sarah called after him that he was to mind and not go on the roof, but to leave that to Peter. With a 'Right ye are' Willie went out into the sunshine.

Meanwhile on the road approaching the cottage, unseen by Peter and Willie, were two girls dressed more or less in Highland costume. One of them was doing all the talking while the other punctuated the speech with inane giggles. The talker was Mrs McTweed's niece Ivy.

'Here, Bella, thon must be ma auntie's wee cottage. Ma mother said she heard it was at the side of a wood at the corner of a field. Jings, she's gettin' somethin' done to 'er roof. Ah always said she had a slate loose. Ah'm sayin' Ah always said——'

She broke off while Bella, appreciating the remark, giggled obligingly.

They came nearer. 'Help ma Rubbert!' exclaimed Ivy, 'Kilroy's here! Look—big Sapsie McFlannel on the roof thonder!' She lifted up her voice and yelled, 'Hullo, Peter!'

Peter, not quite at home even on low roofs like this one, took a hurried look in the direction of the voice, steadied himself and called back politely, 'Hullo, Ivy.'

Then Ivy caught sight of Peter's father on *terra firma* looking very busy as he ostensibly held the steps rigid in case Peter should suddenly wish to descend.

'Oh, you're there forbye, Mr McFlannel. Are you haudin' the steps up, or are they haudin' you up?'

Willie, who did not share his family's dim view of the irrepressible Ivy, answered affably enough that he was holding the steps up for Peter.

'Me and ma pal Bella here was wantin' to see ma auntie,' explained Ivy as they drew near the door, 'can ye let us by?'

'Jist a meenit, then, tae Ah shift the steps f'ae forenent the door,' said Willie. 'The wife an' Maisie's in.'

Ivy stopped. 'Oh, are they?' she exclaimed. 'Well, there's no hurry for ye shiftin' the steps. Bella an' me 'll jist sit doon at the gate thonder.'

Willie surveyed their retreating spread of pleated tartan. 'Ah see yez are dressed fur the hikin'. Whaur's yer rucksacks?'

'Och, we're no' goin' hikin',' replied Ivy as she and Bella spread their kilted skirts over a large part of the garden wall. 'We jist pit on wur kilts an' wur brothers' boots seein' we wur tae be walkin' in the wilds o' the country.'

In the still air her penetrating voice reached Peter clearly and he responded, ' The outskirts of Milngavie are hardly the wilds of the country.'

' Oh, are they no' ? Whit aboot you takin' us fur a walk when ye're done, well ? '

' No, thanks.'

' Doin' yer Boy Scout good deed the day ? '

' Something of the kind.'

' My, my—fair tumblin' ower 'is wulkies tae be pally wi' us, in't 'e, Bella ? ' Bella giggled. ' He'll be scared 'is maw sees 'im speakin' tae me. Look at 'im—sittin' astride the roof thonder like a wee lawdie on a widden horse. Gee-up, horsie ! '

Something of Peter's embarrassment made itself apparent even to Willie who called, ' Heh, Ivy, Ah could shift thae steps an' let ye by intae the hoose.'

' Oh, it's a'right, Mr McFlannel. Bella an' me's havin' the time o' wur lifes sittin' here—sure we are, Bella ! ' Her companion responded with her usual inanity. ' Ah never thocht Mulguy had sichna grand view ! '

' You should see the sights from up here ! ' called Peter.

' Meanin' Bella an' me in wur kilts, eh ? Maybe ye better turn the ither wey, son, in case ye fa' aff yer perch wi' nerves. An' whit wid yer mother dae then fur somethin' tae pit in the pram ? '

' We havenae got a pram ! ' interposed Willie.

' It's a'right, Mr McFlannel. Ah wis jist tryin' fur tae stick a pin in Peter tae see if onything bar sawdust wid come oot.'

Uncomprehending, Willie suggested once again that the new arrivals should announce themselves to their hostess. ' Yer auntie'll be wonderin' whit's keepin' ye,' he added.

' Oh, don't bother yer bunion aboot me, Mister ! Ma auntie disnae know Ah'm comin'.'

' She's bound to know,' shouted Peter ; ' those kilts of yours are shrieking to high heaven—to say nothing of your conversation.'

' Huh—sarcastic gettin', are ye ? ' She turned to her friend. ' Ah don't think he likes wur kilts, Bella.'

' No, *nor* your conversation ! ' came the retort from the roof.

' My-my ! D'ye tell me that ! Ah'm a' cut ! '

For a moment or two there was silence, during which Willie began to feel pinpricks of embarrassment on his own account. He stood back from the door to get a good view of his son: 'Heh, Peter, are ye sure ye widnae like me tae gie ye a haun up there? Ah'm jist staunin' here coontin' ma fing-ers.'

'It's all right, Dad. I'm getting along fine. Just you stay where you are and see the sights.'

'Less o' yer lip, Sapsie!' The rebuke came from the region of the gate. 'You watch yersel.' Walkin' on the roof like that needs white san'shoes.'

'Would you like to come up and hold my hand?' asked Peter.

'Hold yer hand? Nae fear. When Ah want to know what a deid fish feels like Ah'll get the len' o' one at the fish-supper shop.'

Peter, suddenly engrossed with his task, suggested that he would, after all, accept his father's offer of help. Then stiffly Willie made the ascent, while Ivy carried on a running commentary punctuated by the giggles of her friend. Just as Willie's head reached the edge of the slates Peter exclaimed, 'Oh, Dad, I forgot! You promised Mother you wouldn't come on to the roof!'—a statement that drew forth from Ivy a song of her own composition:

'Don't forget you promised Mother,
Don't forget she's watching you!'

She resumed the running commentary:

'That's the stuff, auld yin! Up ye go! Mind yer feet on the lobby lamp! Oopsadaisy! Over the top an' the best o' luck! How does it feel tae be out on the tiles, Mr McFlannel?' she called.

Suddenly her voice dropped to a whisper: 'Here, Bella, come on an' we'll pinch thae steps f'ae the door. Quick! Theym up on the roof there are that busy watchin' the auld yin disnae fa' they'll never see us!'

Their bodies bent and their kilts taking the lines of ostrich's tails, they reached the steps, folded them, and, avoiding the window whence a stream of conversation flowed, they carried them to a ditch at the side of the house. Taking up a fresh point of vantage behind a hedge Ivy burst out into whispered speech again :

'My, whitna pant there's gonnae be ! Oh here, the auld yin musta ta'en cauld feet—he's slitherin' doon the slates again. Here, Ah'm beginnin' tae wish we hadnae of put on wur kilts efter a'—we'll get spotted a' the readier. Keep in yer backshop a bit, Bella !'

While Bella strove to comply with instructions, Willie felt blindly for the top of the steps with his feet. Failing to locate them he blamed his son for having shifted them.

'How could I ?' was the retort. 'I've been here all the time. You must've kicked them away yourself when you came up.'

'Ah never !' Then, turning round he saw the unadorned wall. 'Here—it's thae lassies. They're away—they must've ta'en the steps wi' them.'

'Shout for Mother,' ordered Peter, and the suggestion called forth the remark from Ivy in the hedge : 'Huh—Mammy's tumphy !'

'Serah !' yelled Willie.

'She'll never hear you, Dad ! The window's at the back of the cottage and the door's shut !'

'Ay—an' they'll a' be gabblin' like jucks wantin' their denner ! *Serah ! Maisie !*'

Peter scanned the horizon from his grandstand view by the chimneys. 'These two bizzums can't be far away, Dad. By crickey, I'll wring their necks for them !'

'Could we no' dreep it ?' queried Willie.

'I could, but you're not to risk it, Dad ! See—move over a bit and let me past you.'

'Ah cannae move ! The wire's twisted roon ma ankle. *Heh, Serah !*'

In a moment or two the pair of them had become thoroughly entangled with the wire, greatly to the amusement of the damsels in the offing. Exasperated, Peter yelled, ' Mother !'

'That's right, son,' whispered Ivy, 'a boy's best friend is 'is mother !'

'*Serah! Mrs McTweed!*' called Willie. 'Aw help, Ah'm takin' cramp in ma foot an' Ah cannae get onywhere tae stamp it !'

'Keep still, Dad, or you'll maybe fall over.'

'Whit aboot yellin' doon the lum ?'

As Peter scrambled over the slates to carry out this instruction the ladies in the kitchen of the cottage were preparing the meal. Muffled by soot, Peter's call came down the chimney, 'Mother ! Maisie !'

'What was that ?' exclaimed Sarah in alarm.

'Oh my gosh !' Mrs McTweed clutched the neck of her pullover. 'Don't say the hoose is haunted !'

'Maybe it was a fall of bricks,' was Maisie's suggestion.

'Maisie ! Help ! We're marooned up here !' The words may have been distinct enough when they left Peter's mouth, but the only sense they conveyed by the time they reached the kitchen was the fact that Peter was calling something.

'The fiend !' said Maisie, returning to her task of taking eatables out of paper bags and putting them on plates.

'Oh, what a relief !' Sarah too was clutching her neckband. 'I thought it was a ghost.'

'So did Ah. Ah'm sayin' so did Ah !'

'Maisie, come out and help us !' Peter's words were unrecognisable.

'I say,' said Maisie, 'let's lie low. If they're trying to scare us out of our wits, they'll soon stop if we keep quiet.'

'What's he saying, though ?' Sarah wanted to know.

'Mother !' called Peter.

Mrs McTweed giggled. 'You're right, Maisie, he's trying fur tae pull wur legs—shoutin' murder like that. Of course Peter wis aye yin fur practical jokes. D'ye mind, Mrs McFlannel, the wey he used tae pit squeebs in the keyholes when he wis a wee chap ?'

'Oh dear, will I ever forget the scrapes he used to get into !'

There was more pleasure than pain, though, in Sarah's memory at the safe distance of twenty years.

' Mother ! *Mother !* ' The pitch of Peter's voice was getting higher.

' Oh, don't overdo the murder gag, chum ! ' retorted Maisie.

' D'ye mind,' asked Mrs McTweed, ' the time him an' 'is pals pitched a tent on the top o' the washin'-hooses ? '

' Yes,' Sarah was enjoying herself again, ' with bits of old carpet and waxcloth and coal bags ! '

' Ay—an' whit they had nae use fur they jist stuffed doon the washin'-hoose chimneys ! My, manys a time Ah lost ma temper wi' them—the wee deils ! '

' I seem to remember back-court concerts—' Maisie's contribution was interrupted by a further cry from the fireplace. ' Oh, go and tear brown paper. D'you remember, Mother, we once had a concert in the back court, and we got somebody's piano hurled outside for the occasion. . . .'

Meanwhile on the roof father and son gazed at each other in an agony of frustration.

' Is there nae skylight wundae ? ' moaned Willie.

Peter peered over the other side of the roof and reported there was nothing of the kind.

' Is it as faur tae dreep at the back as it is at the front ? '

Once again Peter reconnoitred, returning with the report that there was a pile of rubbish at one corner of the cottage, so Willie, travelling in a seated position, made the journey over the slates, muttering threats against the conspirators in the hedge, the ' cleckin' o' weemin' in the kitchen and all females in general. When the descent had been negotiated *via* the rubbish heap, he dusted himself and surveyed the landscape for the employment of some of the war-time strategy he had learnt in the Home Guard. From ground level the hedge failed as a screen for those vivid kilts. Proposing that they should work round by the edge of the field in a pincer movement, father and son got down to their manoeuvres.

Unable to see what was happening, Ivy became uneasy. She

even went so far as to say that she didn't like the look of things and them so quiet. ' Where can thae men of went to ? ' she puzzled. ' There musta been a door at the back efter a'.' Then, hearing a sudden commotion at the front door, she turned in that direction and exclaimed, ' Bella, here's the Land Airmy comin' oot tae look fur their cooshy doos ! '

Bella's giggle was not loud enough to drown Sarah's voice as she called, ' Willie ! Peter ! Where are you ? '

Maisie's voice came clearly to them, ' They must've gone round the back—the steps are away.'

' But there's naethin' at the back by's the midden ! ' said Mrs McTweed. ' Ah'm sayin'——.'

' Where can they be ? ' The situation brought out all that was potential in Sarah. ' There's no sign of them anywhere ! '

' I wonder,' pondered Maisie aloud, ' what they were trying to tell us when they were shouting down the chimney ? '

The three of them scattered in all directions just as Ivy suddenly became aware of a sense of urgency on her left flank. She caught sight of the ex-Home Guardsman dragging himself along the ditch, his mouth open. At the same moment Bella caught sight of Peter approaching from the other direction, and any powers of speech she may have possessed were thereby nullified. Realising their danger they unanimously left the hedge and took to the open road, racing past the gate to which the three women were now running with one accord.

Unable to do more than shout, Willie called to the three at the gate, ' Catch them ! They've pinched Mrs McTweed's steps ! '

The spreading kilts were plain to be seen as the girls leapt over a dyke into a field ; but as far as the women could judge, their progress was not impeded by any household equipment. Suddenly the air was rent by two piercing cries and the Highland costumes changed direction. The reason was revealed the next instant.

' Oh ! bulls ! ' shrieked Sarah as two animals, their horns lowered, loped swiftly after the flying figures whose skirts now seemed to be unrelieved red.

Mrs McTweed screamed with laughter. ' That's the best Ah've seen ! Thae's no' bulls—they're coos ! '

Willie and Peter joined in the hilarity, the former mopping his brow as he exclaimed :

' My, whitna pant ! It wis worth while gettin' stuck up on that roof fur the sake o' seein' thae lassies on the run ! '

CHAPTER 9

PETER'S LATEST FAD

I

MAISIE was coming home one evening when she encountered her uncle on the last flight of stairs leading to the flat. She wanted to know if the reason for his standing position was that he was finding the stairs too much for him on account of his corns. He admitted that his feet were none too comfortable.

'Why don't you do something about them?' she asked. 'You've been complaining about those corns for years.'

'Aw, don't turment me, Maisie. Ye'll maybe have corns yersel' some day.'

'I've got one already!'

The man brightened up immediately and offered to sell her a corn cure for only half a crown. When she pointed out that he himself was not much of an advertisement for his wares he retorted that that was different and would she really buy it?

'No, never mind. I believe you'd try to sell milk to a cow, Uncle Matt!'

'Ach, Maisie, ye're jist tryin' fur tae make a fool o' me!'

The girl laughed. 'Peter would tell you I was just about fifty years too late to do that.'

'Ach away, Maisie, ye're no' as auld as that, are ye? My, ye're gettin' on!'

Since it was impossible to tell whether he was being serious or not she decided to laugh it off and they continued the ascent together. While they were waiting for the door to be opened in response to their knock, she asked if this were a social call or if he had an ulterior motive.

'Ach, Maisie, Ah never met onybody like you fur usin' big words. That's the worst o' you bein' a teacher.'

The door opened and Sarah viewed her brother-in-law with a certain lack of cordiality, while Maisie informed her that she was not sure whether he was paying a visit or a visitation.

'Come in,' said Sarah, 'but we're not needing anything to buy.'

Mattha stepped inside. 'Ach, Serah, ye'd think Ah never came up fur tae see yez withoot sellin' ye somethin'.'

'And do you?'

His reply was lost in the heartiness with which his brother came forward and welcomed him, taking him into the kitchen while Maisie went off to her own room to take off hat and coat. The sight of a strange young man sitting by the fireside rather took Mattha by surprise.

'This is a friend of Peter's—Mr M'Gauze,' said Sarah, who, presumably in order to remove all doubts that might exist in the stranger's mind as to the relationship, added, 'This is Mr McFlannel's brother!'

'How d'you do,' said the young man politely.

'Fine, thanks,' replied Mattha literally, 'if it wisnae fur ma corns. Ah'm bothered wi' them somethin' terrible. Ah've got yin on ma wee tae——'

'That'll do, Mattha!' commanded Sarah. 'Mr M'Gauze doesn't want to hear all about your aches and pains. Here, take this chair.'

Mattha took it, heaving a sigh of relief and informing the company in general that he had been on the flat of his feet all day. To prevent further anatomical details, the hostess apologised to the stranger for the fact that he was being kept waiting so long for Peter's return.

'It's quite all right, Mrs McFlannel. I don't mind waiting. Is—ehm—did Maisie not come in just now?'

'Yes, she's away into her room to take off her things.' Really, thought Sarah, he's an awful nice young man, so polite and well spoken. How have I never heard of him before? That is the second time he's asked about Maisie!

'Hoo's hur an' the meenister chap gettin' on?' asked Mattha bluntly.

'I'm sure I don't know what you're talking about,' replied Sarah.

'What minister is this?' The query came from the stranger.

'Their ain meenister!' answered Mattha. 'Ah seen 'er makin' sheep's eyes at 'im at Matt's waddin'.'

'You never did!' Sarah was furious and unaccountably anxious to let the young man know how things stood.

'You don't mean our Mr M'Crepe?'

'Oh, Mr M'Gauze, don't you pay any attention to anything that man says. He just opens his mouth and puts his foot in it.'

Willie, sensing his wife's annoyance, added, 'Ay, corns an' a'!'

Somewhat belatedly, Mattha removed his cap.

'Here, don't put it on the table!' snapped Sarah, making a dive for the headgear. 'I don't like it on the table with the bread and things for Peter's supper.'

'Ach, ma bunnet widnae come tae nae hairm fur a' the wee while Ah'll be here.'

'I didn't mean that!'

'Whit are ye traivellin' fur the night?' asked Willie. 'Grand pianas or Jews harps?'

While Mattha was in the act of denying the suggestion of ulterior motives in his visit, the door opened and Maisie came into the kitchen. Without waiting for a formal introduction, Mr M'Gauze got to his feet.

'Good evening, Maisie. I don't think you remember me, but Peter introduced us the night you looked in at the Youth Club. Bill M'Gauze is the name.'

'Oh, yes, I remember.' Maisie shook hands, since there was no reason for refusing the outstretched palm of Mr M'Gauze. Then, to cover the confusion that existed only in her own mind, Sarah suggested that Maisie should help her to set the supper table for the whole company. In the midst of this operation Peter arrived.

' Hullo, Bill,' exclaimed Peter, ' what are you doing here ? Did I promise to meet you ? '

' No. I wanted to see you before next Club night.'

' Hullo, Mother. What's cookin', good-lookin' ? '

' Liver and fried potatoes ! '

From being a disinterested spectator Willie suddenly roared, ' Liver, did ye say ? Whit wey did Ah no' get ony fur ma tea ? '

' I only got a wee bit from the butcher—not enough for everybody.'

' Well, I like that ! Giein' it tae Peter that disnae ken the difference between liver an' a velvet waistcoat—an' giein' me macaroni an' cheese fur ma tea ! '

' Go on, Mother ! Tell him he's got nothing in his head but his stomach ! It's your line, you know ! '

Mr M'Gauze joined in the laughter and then said, ' Speaking about lines, Peter, I've come up to ask if you'll help us out with a play the Youth Club is putting on.'

' Good gracious ! ' Maisie gaped at him in amazement. ' I hope you only want Peter to make the noises-off ! '

Peter's speech had long been a sore point with Maisie who could get as irritated with the lad's drawling triphthongs as with her father's broad dialect, but Mattha, who could not be expected to appreciate her distinctions, commented that he liked wee plays, especially Scotch ones and what was it called ?

' It's a skit on *In Town Tonight*,' explained Bill.

' Well, here's hoping you didn't want to cast Peter as an announcer ! ' laughed Maisie. ' With that awful Glasgow accent——'

Willie jumped in to defend his son. ' There's naethin' wrang wi' the wey he speaks. If he had oor Mattha's Glasgow accent...'

' Me ? ' Mattha was suitably insulted. ' Ah have nut a Glasgow accent ! It's the folks that stey oot Kelvinside way that has an accent. Ah jist speak plain.'

Bill outlined the plot of the one-act play—which he had apparently written himself—while they were having supper, coaxing Peter to take part in it by insisting that since the action would ostensibly take place in a broadcasting studio he could read his script and avoid the task of memorising his lines. Looking at Bill sitting there enthusing over his project, Sarah thought he was a most attractive young man, well, maybe not as young as Mr M'Crepe, but at any rate he was attractive.

'All the parts are being played by the lads,' Bill was saying, 'I've got a dowager duchess!' Was it her imagination, thought Sarah, or was he really looking especially intently at Maisie as he spoke? 'You see, I've got an idea about this—it's placed in a period twenty years from now, and I expect by then the old aristocracy will be so impoverished by taxes and things that they'll have to earn a livelihood for themselves.'

'Jeengs!' exclaimed Mattha through a mouthful of food. 'Ah thocht it wis jist teachers that went in fur big words.'

'Never heed him, Bill!' said Peter. 'Tell us about the dowager duchess.'

'Well, she's opened a boarding-house for unemployed dress-makers. By that time, of course, so much cloth will have been exported to meet our succession of economic crises that dress-makers will have nothing to work on.'

'I see!' Maisie seemed to be sharing his enthusiasm. 'Speaking about dressmakers, what style of clothes will the characters be wearing?'

'Oh, very shabby nineteen-forty-seven.'

'Mn! What other characters have you?'

'Oh, a beauty specialist. Women won't be powdering their noses in nineteen-sixty-seven, so the talk by the beauty specialist will be about how to make noses shine!'

Just to show she was taking an intelligent interest in the conversation, Sarah asked if this was going to be a comic play. Bashfully the old-young man said he had his hopes. His manner took on a touching modesty when Maisie insisted that it was going to be a scream, and what else was there?

'Well, there's to be the mannish type of female who specialises in dogs. Oh—and instead of smoking, all the characters take snuff.'

'What! The duchess as well?' Sarah looked her bewilderment.

'Of course not! She's old-fashioned, Mrs McFlannel! She chews gum!'

The literal Sarah said, 'Well, I must say I never heard of a duchess that did that! I was reading an awful nice story in the *Companion* where——'

'But, Mother, this is supposed to be a farce!' explained Maisie-the-teacher-who-was-paid-to-correct-mistakes.

'Have ye no' got a wee coamic in it?' queried Mattha.

'Not a *wee* comic!' replied the playwright, 'but I've got a huge labourer from the Salvage Department who comes to the studio in his working clothes and gives a chance for a crack about the bad smell from the programme.'

'You *are* having an announcer, aren't you?' Maisie's interest was perfectly genuine, and sitting there with her eyes shining like that, she was obviously putting ideas into Bill M'Gauze's head, if indeed, her mother reflected, they were not there already.

'Actually this character's got to be both producer and announcer. Frightfully cultured voice. Oh—and there'll be notices plastered all over the place "No Snuffing during Transmission."'

'Imagine that!' was Mattha's mournful observation. 'Ah've had three transmissions. Hale three pints o' bluid.'

Gently Maisie asked if by any chance he meant transfusions.

Willie expressed disgust. 'Ach, Ah cannae mak' heid nor tail o' this conversation. One meenit ye're talkin' aboot a stage play an' the next meenit it's the wireless.'

It was fully eleven o'clock before Bill and Mattha showed any sign of going to their respective homes. Mattha, apparently under the impression that his blood-relationship entitled him to outstay the other, was among those who said goodnight to him at the door. With a promise to send Peter a copy of the play and assuring him that the part would fit him like a glove, Bill tore himself away. When the door had closed, Maisie turned to her brother and said, 'I say, Peter, he's pulling your leg about the part fitting you like a glove. That Glasgow drawl of yours would make the whole thing ridiculous.'

'You shut up about my Glasgow drawl! Your own speech isn't consistent.'

'Maybe, but I'm not to be walking on to a stage acting the part of an announcer—he said himself it was a cultured voice!'

Sarah took up the cudgels for Peter. 'I don't see anything wrong with the way Peter speaks, but could he not go to a teacher for elocution lessons?'

Willie laughed. 'Heh, Mattha, could you no' sell 'im an elocution teacher?'

'Naw! But Ah could sell 'im a book Ah picked up at the barras the day aboot public speaking. Ah thocht it might come in handy if ever Ah got a barra o' ma ain—ye know—sellin' toffee aipples—they say there's a termedious profit in theym.'

'You're a wee marvel, Uncle Matt!' exclaimed Maisie banteringly. 'Have you got the book with you?'

Mattha drew the volume from his pocket with a sidelong look at the student of refined speech. 'It'll cost ye three an' nine'ms, Peter.'

Peter took it, turned it round, smelt it, flicked the pages over and then exclaimed, 'What's this on the back page—fourpence?'

'Well, ehm—'—Mattha searched the floor for self-justification—'Ah had ma time traivellin' tae the barras an' back. It's a bargain if ye jist knew it. Look, it tells ye a' aboot hoo tae staun' on a platform at a meetin' an' when tae fling oot yer haun' an' a' that kinna thing.'

Handing the book back, Peter said that he would prefer something more modern, and Sarah, feeling that he was making a mistake, suggested that what was good for the orators of the past was surely good enough for those of the present day.

'Yes, but, Mother, Peter's not going to be an orator—he's going to be an announcer!' Maisie pointed out.

Willie added, 'Ay—jist like ye aye wanted 'im tae be!' When Sarah assured him that she had got over that notion he went on, 'Ah mind when Ah wis a wee chap at the Bandyhope

Ah used tae recite a pome aboot a wee Jimmy Dooglas that wis cairryin' a piece tae a man that wis hidin——'

Anxious to ingratiate himself and his wares, Mattha said, ' Ay—Ah mind it an' a', Wullie. Awful touchin' it wis ! ' Then suddenly observing Peter having another surreptitious squint at the volume, he insisted that if he was getting information out of it, he would have to pay the purchase price of three shillings and ninepence.

' Just a minute, Uncle Matt. Listen to this, folk. It says here : " For effective public speech a black velvet jacket with a tasteful waistcoat in subdued colours is advisable." It doesn't say anything about trousers. D'you think short khaki pants would do, Maisie ? '

The young folk laughed together while Sarah, unheeded, told them not to be vulgar. Instead they put their heads together and examined the text more closely, a posture which brought from the salesman the opinion that they ought to ' go haufers ' with the payment. Ignoring him, Maisie laughed again and said, ' Here's more of it. " A chaste, concise and energetic style is more effective than a florid, turgid and prolix one ; so the judicious employment of moderate gesture is more effective than any possible amplification of spasmodic attitudes or redundancy of facial changes." What d'you think of that ! '

' Ach—you teachers ! ' sneered Mattha, feeling that due respect was not being paid to the book. ' You an' yer big words ! Ye jist made that up as ye went along. Nae book wid put onything so daft as that in it.'

She shoved it under his nose, urging him to read for himself. Declining the offer, he said, ' D'ye no' want it, well ? '

' It'll be more use to you, Uncle Matt ! ' said Peter.

' Ach—a' thae big words wid be nae use fur toffee aipples. Tuppence doon the stank, that's whit it is ! '

' Just the one tuppence ? ' asked Maisie sweetly.

He edged nearer the door. ' Ah better be gettin' hame. The wife 'll be wonderin' whit's came ower me. Oh, ma corns ! Whitna tribulation corns is ! '

'Did ye never think o' takin' up horseback ridin' ? ' asked Willie.

'Don't be daft ! ' Mattha was scornful. 'Hoo could Biddy an' me keep a horse in a room-an'-kitchen up a close.' Pocketing his tuppence-worth, he hirpled out of the house and down the stair leaving behind him no clear idea of the purpose of his visit.

2

Once Peter had made up his mind to equip himself for the part of the announcer in Bill M'Gauze's play he submitted meekly to Maisie's constant correction of his drawling speech, and finally consented to allow her to ask the advice of the Speech Training Mistress who visited her school. The result was that, furnished with a modern book on the subject, Peter shut himself in the parlour with it, and faint noises could be heard in the still of the evening : ' Rib bone, rib bone, solemn moment, solemn moment, bite tongue, bite tongue. . . .'

One day Peter, not realising the enormity of the suggestion, asked Maisie if she thought the Reverend Mr M'Crepe could give him any assistance with the pronunciation of tricky works like ' gas ' and ' Africa.'

'Why ask me ? ' demanded Maisie. 'I haven't seen him for weeks ! '

Sarah, overhearing the answer, said within herself, ' Oh, Maisie, and you twice at church on Sunday ! '

'Okay, okay,' said Peter, 'I was only asking. " Once more unto the breach, dear friends, once more . . ." '

The monologues continued into the night, so that Sarah was forced to get out of bed and plead with the lad, for the sake of the neighbours, to reduce the volume of his exercises.

'Sorry, Mum,' he said contritely, ' the trouble is—I don't want to make a fool of the announcer part in this play. But Bill should be up with the script tomorrow night, so you won't have much longer to put up with the shouting.'

Sarah stole back to bed. Bill coming to the house tomorrow night ? Why did Mr M'Crepe never put in an appearance—

they had had such a happy evening together the last time he called and she had been in bed ! Oh well. . . .

When Bill arrived Peter hastened to assure him that he had been at some pains to equip himself for the part.

' But I told you, old man,' said Bill, ' you're just right for the part as you are ! '

Bashfully Peter said, ' Ugh away ! ' while Bill paid his respects to the rest of the family and Sarah watched carefully.

Just as carefully, to show how thoroughly he had been practising good speech, Peter asked to see the script of the play. Bill produced it with a twinkle in his eye, thumbing over the typewritten pages. ' Here you are,' he said, indicating a spot on the script, ' here's your cue line. Want to read it over ? '

Peter cleared his throat and started in on it : ' " Yes, sir, I was brung up in the Port Dundas district of Glasgow, and used to fish for baggies in the canawl when I was a child." '

He stared at his friend. ' Bill,' he said gently, ' I hope you don't think I'm interfering, but no announcer would speak like that ! '

' Maybe they will in 1967, though,' suggested Maisie, apparently taking sides with Bill.

But he, putting back his head and laughing, said, ' Peter, you mutt ! It's not the announcer's part you're to play ! It's the scavenger's ! I told you—your speech is dead right for it ! '

And Willie, glad that for once the critical faculties of the younger generation were turned away from him, whistled for the dog and went for a walk.

CHAPTER 10

HIGHLAND FLING

I

AFTER a week or so, during which Peter readjusted his ideas and got down to the study of his part, life continued its uneventful placidity. Beds had to be made, clothes had to be washed, shopping had to be done, children had to be taught and ships had to be built. And then, out of the blue, came a diversion. A distant relation of Sarah's wrote to say that he was coming to Glasgow to visit a friend who was having treatment in one of the hospitals, and could she put him up for a day or two. She poured out her worries to her neighbour Mrs M'Corduroy while they were both engaged cleaning their door-steps.

' I just don't know what I'll give him to eat,' complained Sarah.

' Don't worry—he'll be bringing you a crate of eggs and a haunch of venison.'

' Oh, they're not well off, poor souls. But they've got a cow—I wish he could bring me some milk. That's my worst shortage besides potatoes.'

' Oh, potatoes ! Who would ever 've thought we'd have been rationed for them ? '

' Another thing that's worrying me is—the noise ! I'm afraid he'll not sleep, poor old man, after the quietness of Mull.'

Mrs M'Corduroy tried to comfort her. ' Well, one thing, thanks to Countess McMuslin on the top flat, we've all been trained to make no noise after eleven o'clock at night.'

' Oh, I know the tenement itself is quiet enough—it's the traffic in the street I was thinking about. Maisie's going to sleep in the spare bedroom so's to let him have her room at the back.'

' Well, here's hoping the dustmen don't pay their weekly visit while he's here ! Did you hear them last night ? I think they were playing tennis with the ashbins.'

Sarah said she hadn't heard them.

' What, they nearly wakened the dead ! Dear only knows what Countess McMuslin said to the Cleansing Department on the phone this morning.'

' Shsh ! ' said Sarah, starting to scrub her doorstep all over again, ' here she's coming down the stair.'

Mrs M'Corduroy, however, was not in the least abashed. ' Oh, good morning, Mrs McMuslin,' she boomed, ' I'm just saying to Mrs McFlannel that we'll have to complain about the dustmen's noise through the night.'

Sarah, who had not encountered her face to face since the night that she and Willie had gone to investigate the noise overhead, was anxious to save the lady any embarrassment, so she continued to scrub a piece of wood already sparklingly white. But Mrs McMuslin had apparently forgotten the incident, for she said quite composedly to Mrs M'Corduroy that she had already telephoned a complaint.

' Oh,' said Mrs M'Corduroy, ' and what did they say ? '

' I didn't give them the chance to say anything. I put down the receiver as soon as I had said all I wanted to ! '

' Oh—what *did* you say ? '

Sarah stopped scrubbing to listen. ' I told them,' said Mrs McMuslin in her precise diction, ' that there was a bye-law against making noises after eight o'clock at night, and that I intended to see that it was kept.'

' I thought it was just that you couldn't beat your rugs after eight o'clock,' put in Sarah.

' If it's wrong to beat rugs after eight o'clock, then it's wrong to make any other noise ! ' insisted Mrs McMuslin. ' I'm taking the matter up with the police. I simply must have silence after I go to bed. My nerves won't stand noise.'

'When *do* you go to bed ? ' asked Mrs M'Corduroy.

'Ten o'clock every night without fail.'

Wiping off the soap-suds she had so unnecessarily created, Sarah remarked that people who could get to bed as early as ten o'clock were extremely fortunate.

'Huh ! ' was Mrs M'Corduroy's observation, ' at ten o'clock my husband and I are so fed up with the sight of each other that we want to start throwing things,' a statement that horrified Sarah by its inaccuracy. Mrs McMuslin, however, took it literally.

'Well, all I can say is—if you make a disturbance after ten o'clock I shall be compelled to report the matter to the factor. He is my brother, you know. Good morning ! ' and she went down the stairs leaving the other two agape. Once she was out of earshot Mrs M'Corduroy exclaimed : ' Whew ! What a wet Sunday at the coast ! '

'Oh dear-dear ! I better get Peter to oil our pulleys. It would be terrible if she got us put out of our house for that ! '

2

Willie had gone to the station to meet the arriving guest, and now he had convoyed him as far as the stairway leading to the McFlannel flat. The two men carried between them a large and exceedingly heavy trunk, the weight of which made Willie pech out, ' Ye'll be feelin' the stairs wi' you being' used wi' a low door in Mull.'

Without a trace of a pech and in a lovely soft Highland accent the elderly man replied that he was very well accustomed to climbing.

'Oh, ye mean sclimmin' hills lookin' fur sheep ? ' Willie's pause might have appeared to the casual observer to be a courteous anxiety to hear the answer to his question, but the man from Mull had a gleg eye.

'There wass no need for you to be carrying my trunk. I could easily have carried it as well as my suitcase. Give it to me.'

Willie declined to do so, took another appraising glance at

the article in question, and asked if the visitor was thinking of staying long.

But all the satisfaction he got was, 'I will be considering the matter.'

'Ye'll find Glasgow a gey change f'ae yer ain wee village,' said Willie, just to show he still had breath for conversation.

'There iss no village where my croft iss. My nearest neighbour lives farther up the glen about seven miles away.'

'Huh,' panted Willie, 'oor nearest neebur's aboot seeven feet away!' The landing reached at last, he rang or rather hung on to the bell-pull. With a sudden access of honesty he panted, 'Oh my, Ah must be gettin' auld—thae stairs jist aboot knocks me sideweys. Unless it wis your trunk, man. Ye didn't need tae bring yer mangle, ye ken.'

'I do not understand you,' was the frank reply. 'I have no mangle.'

'Ach, forget it!' urged Willie, hearing the welcome sound of someone coming to open the door. It was Peter, whose welcome was reinforced by Sarah who came forward immediately. While the general speeches of hospitality were still being made, Willie wanted to know if he should put the heavy trunk in Maisie's room, and when he had been assured that the room was at his sole disposal Mr McPlaid gave his consent for the miniature pantechnicon to be carried thither.

This drew Sarah's attention to the extraordinary quantity of luggage lying just inside the door and she could not refrain from exclaiming, 'Dear me, Mr McPlaid, you'd think you were here for a month!'

'I will be considering the matter,' was the guarded reply, then he added, 'My wife gave me a parcel to give to you.'

Sarah thanked him, ordered her husband and son to show the stranger where he could wash, saw to the dragging of the heavy trunk and suitcase into the guest-room, and then ran to the scullery where she reported the matter to Maisie.

'Cheer up, Mother,' said the girl, 'he's brought you a parcel—it's sure to be eggs.'

Then while the pair of them were conjuring up visions of

the large quantity of eggs that could be accommodated in the luggage, Peter arrived on the scene saying, ' Here's the parcel, Mum ! '

Sarah opened her eyes at the sight of a crumpled paper bag which, when opened, revealed half a dozen scones.

' And all burnt too ! ' she complained. ' Oh dear-dear, how can I say thank you to him for these ? Are you sure, Peter—I mean—you didn't see anything else ? '

' Well, I couldn't exactly poke my nose into his trunk, could I ? '

' Did you not see any eggs knocking around ? ' asked Maisie.

' No—not even the hen that lays them ! '

' I'm afraid he'll have to eat all these scones himself,' said Sarah, ' for none of you will look at burnt things.'

' I tell you what,' said Maisie, ' we'll tell him we don't want to deprive him of them.'

' Ach, wait till 'e's tasted yours, Serah, an' e'll no' look at thae bent yins ! '

At that the visitor himself came into the kitchen. ' Oh, come away, Mr McPlaid,' said Sarah, ' we're just going to have supper along with you. Did you have a meal on the train ? '

' Yes, I had some of my wife's scones.' He produced a milk bottle and Sarah's smiles broke out, disappearing the next instant as he explained that it was buttermilk for his porridge. ' My wife was sure you would not be giving me the kind of buttermilk I am accustomed to,' he added.

' I have brought some of my wife's cakes,' he went on, placing some more unshapely scones on the table, this time of the oat-meal variety and even more excessively fired than their cousins. ' I will not be eating your food, Mrs McFlannel.'

Realising that the man was eager to spare her any trouble in finding food for him, Sarah remarked that it was very thought-ful of him.

' Are ye rationed fur yer meat in Mull ? ' asked Willie.

' Yes. Oh, I was forgetting ! I have brought a pair of rabbits. I will be fetching them straightaway.' And off he went in the direction of his bedroom.

' I say, Maisie,' whispered Peter, ' the old boy must've brought not only Paw and Maw rabbit, but all the wee weans as well. His trunk's a dead weight.'

' Jeengs ay ! ' put in Willie who was slowly recovering his breathing equanimity, ' Ah wis fair wabbit humphin' it up the stair. He must be traivellin' fur deid sheep an' cairries 'is samples wi' 'im.'

' He doesn't look as though he had the intelligence to travel for anything—not even pleasure,' was Maisie's comment.

' Shsh,' said her mother, ' he'll hear you ! '

' I don't care. Imagine bringing buttermilk for himself ! '

' Ah mind the day when Ah used tae think soor dook wis a rare slockener,' remarked Willie wistfully.

While his daughter was telling him to speak in English if he wanted to be understood, the visitor came back into their midst.

' Here you are, Mistress McFlannel. These two rabbits were running about the slopes of Ben More last evening.'

' Oh, thanks, Mr McPlaid,' said Sarah, ' I'm real glad of them. Only, I'm not sure how to skin them.'

' If you will hang them up by their hind legs I will be skinning them for you in the morning,' said he.

' Oh, thanks very much. Ehm—you'll be wanting to go to your bed pretty early ? ' There was an element of hope about Sarah's query.

' I will be considering the matter,' was the reply.

' D'you not find life awful humdrum at the back of beyond ? ' asked Peter when they were seated round the tea-table.

' Oh, no. We have plenty to amuse us,' said Mr McPlaid with a twinkle in his eye that no-one had noticed earlier. ' In the winter we have the wireless and in the summer we have the hikkers.'

' You mean the hikers, Mr McPlaid ? ' The question could come from one quarter only.

' In my part of the country, Miss McFlannel,' he replied with dignity, ' they are known as hikkers. They always travel in pairs and there are times when we cannot be saying whether they are men or women for they all wear the kilt and none of them knowing how to wear it properly.'

'I've done a bit of hiking myself,' interjected Peter, 'and I don't wear a kilt !'

'I should hope not,' said his sister, 'you haven't the legs for it !'

'In my experience that iss not a point which occurs to hikkers. No, no. We do not find life humdrum, Peter.'

'Come on an' let's get stairtit tae wur supper,' said Willie. 'D'ye like ham an' eggs, Mr McPlaid ?'

'Indeed I do, Mr McFlannel.'

'Well, if we'd had ham, we coulda had ham an' eggs if we'd had eggs.'

'Oh, Dad,' groaned Maisie.

Sarah, to prevent her husband from saying openly that he was looking forward to the taste of Mull eggs, plunged into a query about Mr McPlaid's preferences in the way of tea. That settled, the conversation wore round to the question of sheep dogs and from that to pet dogs in general and Susan in particular. Mr McPlaid admitted that he did not care for Cairn terriers as a rule, but was pleased to see that this was a quiet beast.

'And so she would need to be,' said Sarah, 'considering the kind of woman that lives up above us. She can't bear noise of any kind. That reminds me, Peter, you'll need to oil the pulleys this very night. That woman McMuslin——'

Mr McPlaid got to his feet and interrupted the monologue with the bald statement that he wished to retire for the night. Sarah's relief was disconcerting, but she managed to assure him that she had done all she could for his comfort, putting two hot-water bottles in his bed.

'It is very kind of you, mistress, but I have never been accustomed to such things.'

'Is that so ? Well, just put them on the floor. You know your way about the house ; it's not that big. I hope you'll sleep well. I'll give you a knock in the morning.'

'There is no need. I am accustomed to wakening myself in the morning. Goodnight to you all.'

They all called 'goodnight' in return, Willie having a special rhyming version of his own which was 'Goodnight, sleep tight, don't let the bugs bite.'

'Willie, don't be vulgar!' snapped his wife.

The visitor paused with his hand on the door. 'I am not accustomed to bugs in the bed.'

'Don't worry, Mr McPlaid,' the hostess assured him, 'it's just my husband's idea of a joke.'

'I am not accustomed to jokes of that kind. Goodnight.'

'Will eight o'clock be too early for me to waken you?' she continued.

'I am accustomed to rising every morning at five o'clock.'

Even Willie was shocked at this statement. 'Ach, you—ye're no' at the back o' Benachie noo! Ye've nae rabbits tae chase the morn's morn. Ye better stey in yer bed tae ye're cried.'

'I could be going for a walk in the morning,' persisted the gentleman.

'But it'll be dark,' said Peter; 'you'll get lost!'

'You could go with him,' Maisie prodded her brother.

'Right you are—if you come as well!' he prodded back.

The Head of the house took a strong line. 'There's nane o' yez goin' oot this hoose at five in the mornin'. Jist you stey in yer bed, mister, an' no' be giein' the wife ony bother.'

With a courteous 'I have no wish to be giving trouble to anyone,' the visitor closed the door firmly.

3

There was an instant sigh of relief from all members of the family, especially Sarah who said, 'Oh dear-dear, I'm afraid he's going to be awful difficult to put up with. I wonder how long he's staying?'

'He will be considering it,' imitated Peter. 'All the same, Maisie, the old boy's got a sense of humour.'

'You mean about the hikkers?'

'Sure. Come to think of it, folk in those isolated places

must think town folks are mad if all they see of them is the hiking fraternity.'

While the menfolk sat down to read the evening papers thoroughly, the women cleared the supper-table, washed the dishes, told each other once more that he might have brought something very much less acceptable than two rabbits, considering how fond Susan was of the offal thereof, when suddenly there was a mysterious sound of bumping and creaking.

'Don't worry, Mother,' said Maisie, 'that'll be him putting his bottles out of his bed.'

'Oh, it's worse than that!' maintained Sarah as the noise continued. Willie too was impressed, giving voice to the opinion that he was playing peever with his heavy trunk. When there seemed no indication that the disturbance was ceasing Sarah asked Peter if he couldn't invent an excuse for going into the man's room.

'I know,' said Maisie, 'he's shifting the furniture. I've heard of folk that can only sleep with their heads to the north.'

'You mean,' giggled Peter, 'he will not be accustomed . . .'

Willie said, 'Jeengs, ye'd think he wis barricading himself in!'

'I know,' Peter giggled once more, 'he's got a dead corpse in the trunk and he's scared the police are after him!'

'Peter, don't be vulgar.' The stricture was half-hearted, however, Sarah's mind being one jump ahead, or rather above. 'Oh, dear-dear, what if Mrs McMuslin hears that?'

'Ach you! You let that wumman get in yer hair,' was her husband's comment.

'I can't help it! She makes such a fuss over the least wee noise. She'll complain to the factor about this—he's her brother —and we'll maybe get put out on the street.'

And in that moment there came to them an unearthly wail, like the shriek of the tortured souls who meet in the Great Glen of Mull to terrify the reckless camper by the burn at Torness. And as the scraighs rose in pitch and volume there was added to the eldritchery the terror shrieks of Sarah and the bewitched yapping of Susan the dog.

Willie, however, got up from his seat, his face transformed with delight. ' It's the bagpipes ! ' he yelled, adding to the din.

Sarah turned on him. ' What, the bagpipes ! At this time of the night ! Up a close ! Oh, Susan, be quiet ! '

But the man made for the door. ' He's gonnae gie's a choon ! We'll need tae bring 'im oot so's tae get the full benefit o't.'

There was a scuffle as Sarah clutched at her husband. ' Oh, Willie, stop him ! You must ! Think of the neighbours ! ' Then turning on the dog, she shrieked, ' Be quiet, you ! '

Willie, however, was beyond human intervention. He was no longer a middle-aged foreman plater in a Clydeside shipyard, he was a raw recruit marching, kilt a-swing, to the tune of the ' Black Bear.'

Sarah shook him. " Willie, don't stand there with that silly smile on your face ! Do something ! Shout on him to stop. Oh dear-dear, Mrs McMuslin'll be down any minute.'

' She goes to bed at ten, on her own admission, Mother, and it'll take her a minute or two to make herself presentable,' said Maisie ; but she had to hurry after her mother as she spoke to make sure that what she was saying was heard. She caught up with her at the door whence the deafening din emanated.

' Mr McPlaid ! Mr McPlaid ! ' screamed Sarah, accompanying herself with her fists on the door panels. She tried and failed to open the door ; something large was blocking the way.

' Whit's the use o' yellin' like that ? ' shouted Willie in her ear. ' The man cannae hear ye ! '

' But you're not allowed to play the bagpipes in a tenement after eight o'clock at night ! ' she retorted as she turned to beat a renewed tattoo on the door.

' Heh, stop hammerin' like that ! ' protested her husband. ' The wife up the stair'll hear ye. The man's daein' fine. Ah wish he'd gie us the " Black Bear." '

The noise was terrific, nevertheless there was a quality about the sound of the door-bell which penetrated to Sarah's consciousness, probably because she had been dreading it.

'Oh, there's Mrs McMuslin ! I knew it ! What'll we do ? ' She tried the bedroom door again. 'Mr McPlaid,' she shrieked, ' you'll get us put out of our house ! *Stop that noise.*'

'It's you that's makin' the noise, wumman—no' him ! That's music—it warms the cockles o' yer hert.'

Once again the sound of the door-bell won its way through to the cockles of Sarah's heart. 'Peter,' she called, ' you go. I'm frightened.'

When Peter had obliged it was found to be Mrs M'Corduroy and not Mrs McMuslin who was standing there complaining that she could not get her dog to stop barking, and what was it all about ?

'Come on in,' said Peter, who had a warm affection for the woman ; ' we'll do the Highland Fling together ! '

'I'd be delighted at any other time, Peter,' she replied. Out there on the landing it seemed comparatively quiet, nevertheless she was obviously greatly agitated. 'I must get my dog to stop barking or Mrs McMuslin 'll be down complaining. Is that what's called the skirl of the pipes ? '

Sarah came out on to her door-mat at that. 'Oh, Mrs M'Corduroy, isn't this terrible ! I can't get him to stop. He's got all the furniture piled up behind the door.'

'He must've had a premonition you'd want to wring his neck, Mother,' said Maisie from behind.

'Away wi' ye,' Willie's eyes were radiant with delight, ' he's shifted the furnicher so's tae get room tae march up an' doon while he's playin'. If it's the wife up the stair ye're feart fur, leave'er tae me.'

'I hear Susan's as excited as my dog,' said Mrs M'Corduroy. ' After the way we've trained the wee brutes not to bark—it's too bad. . . . The awkward thing is,' she drew Sarah farther out on to the landing, ' we're—I mean—I'm not anxious to be reported to the factor at the moment, Mrs McFlannel. You see—it's a little matter of the rent.'

In the midst of her mental maelstrom Sarah found peace enough to say sympathetically, 'Oh, I'm awful sorry, Mrs M'Corduroy. Why didn't you tell me before ? '

For some unknown reason the wailing of the pipes fell to a sobbing, then to a sigh, and, with a grunt, to an eerie silence. The dogs, no longer tortured, yelped a few staccato notes and retired from the concert.

It was Willie's turn now to knock on the door. ' Come on oota there, man,' he yelled with unnecessary loudness, ' ye'll get mair room tae march up an' doon the lobby here ! '

' No-no ! ' wailed Sarah. ' He must stop ! '

' We can't have this, you know, Mr McFlannel,' said Mrs M'Corduroy for reasons of her own.

' Ach, haud yer wheesht, the baith o' yez ! '

Once again there was the sound of heavy furniture being dragged hither and thither inside the room, the two dogs, near and far, opened up their artillery again, and in a moment or two Mr McPlaid was in their midst, his moroseness gone, his face as radiant as that of his host as he fondled his pipes and asked if they were enjoying the music. Sarah, whose blood was thin with the limitations of tenement life, repeated the word ' music ' with a hiss. Willie, however, more than made up for her lack of enthusiasm.

' On ye go, man ! ' he urged. ' Gie's——'

' No, Willie ! Not at this time of night ! '

' Away wi' ye, wumman ! ' The ex-Glasgow Highlander gave a little muscular emphasis to his words. ' Come on, Mr McPlaid, gie's the " Black Bear " ! '

As the guest prepared to oblige Mrs M'Corduroy hurried from the scene saying, ' Good grief ! I'll need to go and put a tea-cosy over my dog's ears ! ' On the threshold she bumped into somebody. ' Oh,' she yelped, ' Mrs McFlannel ! Look who's here ! '

Mrs McFlannel looked and beheld the object of her dread.

' Oh, Mrs McMuslin, isn't this awful ! ' she began as though dissociating herself from the piobaireachd. ' I can't tell you how sorry I am ! . . . *Willie : here's Mrs McMuslin !* '

The man, in his happy dwam, turned, nodded affably at the newcomer, saying, ' Hoo'ye, missus. Doon tae hear the music better ? '

'No, no, Willie,' screamed Sarah, 'don't you see? You must make him stop. Mrs McMuslin's the factor's sister !'

'No, please,' shouted Mrs McMuslin, whose face, now that Sarah had a chance to look at it properly, was wearing that same quality of foolishness she observed in her own husband's. 'Don't stop him,' was the astonishing statement, 'I like it !'

Everybody, with the exception of Willie, who was not listening, and Mr McPlaid, who was otherwise engaged, shouted, 'You what ?'

'I like the pipes !' The metamorphosis was unbelievable. Instead of her usual mincing correct speech and genteel manner, Mrs McMuslin was shouting so that even Willie heard her.

'Put it there, missus,' he held out his hand, which she clasped wholeheartedly.

'I was born and brought up in Inverness, and the pipes are my favourite instrument,' she called to them all above the din of the 'Black Bear.' 'They make me feel young and happy again.'

The ceilidh broke up about midnight, and was repeated each evening as long as Mr McPlaid felt his friend required to be visited in hospital. At last the day came when he had to go.

'Goodbye, Mr McPlaid,' said Sarah, seeing him off the premises. 'We've fairly enjoyed your visit. We'll miss the cheery nights we've had with you and the neighbours.'

'And I will be missing the company. You have been very kind to me.' He stood in the lobby, his suitcase at his feet.

'Here,' said Sarah, peering at his luggage, 'are you not taking your trunk ? Do you want me to send it on after you ?'

'No, thank you. She was only an old tin trunk which you will be pleased to keep. She was full of potatoes which I understand you are short of in Glasgow just now.'

'Potatoes !' exclaimed Sarah. 'Oh, isn't that wonderful ! My, that was real kind of you !'

She watched his retreating figure. Really, he was the nicest man. . . .

CHAPTER 11

SOMETHING TO BRAG ABOUT

I

SARAH McFLANNEL was no angel—she had her full quota of human foibles. Chief among her limitations was her incapacity to regard her brother-in-law with affection. The sight of him standing on her door-mat was enough to arouse all her latent suspicions, prejudices and thorough-going dislikes, and when her husband was not there to put the brake on her outspokenness Mattha was in no doubt as to her attitude towards him. It says something for his keen business sense, then, when one forenoon at the beginning of November he was willing to brave the lioness in her den.

' Oh, it's you,' she said coldly when she opened the door to him. ' What are you doing here at this time of the day ? '

' Ach, Ah wis jist passin',' he answered vaguely as he stepped unbidden into the house.

' I'm just hurrying to get out my messages,' was the rather pale echo of a welcome ; ' I hope you're not up to try and sell me something.'

' It never entered ma heid,' he replied adenoidally and un-truthfully. His furtive gaze darted hither and thither. ' My, Serah,' he went on, ' but ye fairly keep a braw hoose. Ah'm aye tellin' the wife.'

' That's enough, Mattha,' replied Sarah non-co-operatively, ' I know fine when you start out like that you're trying to butter me up for something you've got to sell.'

' Ah never said a word aboot sellin'.'

' Maybe not yet—but I know you ! ' They went into the

kitchen, where Mattha, sitting down, contemplated the floor-cloth and commended the polish thereof. 'Are ye no' feart yer coalman 'll skite some day an' skail 'is bag?' he inquired.

'Are you trying to sell me some new floor polish?'

'Ach, Serah, ye're awful suspeecious! Here, speakin' aboot bein' suspeecious—hoo's yer pal M'Cotton gettin' on thae days?'

Sarah turned on him: 'She's no pal of mine, and you know it! Why the sudden interest in her?'

'Oh, nothin',' he answered evasively. Then, his eyes being still bent in the region of the floor, he went on, 'My, but that's an awful quiet wee dug ye've got! Ye never hear a cheep oota its heid. Ye musta trained it awful weel. Does it no' even bark at the postie?'

'No, of course not,' said Sarah, who could not be bothered to explain that Susan was allergic to bagpipes. 'A dog that barks in a tenement is a disgrace to its owners.'

'Ye know, Serah, Ah think you're fair wonderfu'—the wey ye've brung up yer weans an' yer dug an'——'

'Mattha McFlannel, that's enough! You're not getting round me with that kind of balderdash. What is it you want?'

'Ah'm no' wantin' naethin'. Ehm—hoo's Maisie gettin' on? Ony chance o' hur gettin' aff wi' yer new meenister?'

'She's not interested in ministers!' snapped Sarah to the best of her knowledge and belief.

'Is he much o' a preacher?'

'Good gracious, what's come over you that you're suddenly interested in religion?'

'Och, Ah wis jist wonderin'. Whit aboot Peter—is he still fiddlin' away at 'is fiddle?'

'Now and again. He's playing at a Youth Club concert next week.'

'Imagine that! He'll maybe be on the wireless yet! Hoo wid ye like tae hear yer son's playin' comin' oota yer ain wireless set, eh?'

'I would like it fine, but ugh, I don't suppose it'll ever happen.' She slipped up for a moment there and showed a hint of wistfulness that Mattha was quick to seize on.

'Ah widnae be so sure !'

'What would you not be so sure about ?'

'Well, its like this, see. Ah wis mendin' a clock fur a man that works in the BBC, see ?'

'You mean you were tinkering with it,' she commented coldly.

'Well—ehm—' Mattha's manner conveyed the impression that he was willing to let that flea stick to the wall—' this chap wis tellin' me that the BBC's openin' a new club on Saturday —that's the morn—there's tae be a big " do " on. The Lord Provost is daein' somethin' at it.'

'What's this got to do with our Peter playing on the wireless ?'

'Am Ah no' tellin' ye ? It's like this, see. This—ehm— this clock that Ah wis mendin', well, Ah had it a month ago, an' it seems it's no' goin' right yet, an' 'e brung it back an' 'e said 'e wisnae gonnae pey me fur sortin' it again unless it went right fur a hale week. Some folk are right nasty-minded, so they are.'

'He seems to have sized you up all right. Go on.'

'Well, Ah wisnae gonnae be pittin' in ma time mendin' 'is nock fur nothin', so Ah says tae 'im if he liked tae get me some tickets fur this BBC club affair we wid ca' it quits. See ?'

'No, I don't,' she said frankly, ' but go on.'

'So he says it wis only extra special folk that wis allowed at this thing, but he wid see whit he could do. So this mornin' the tickets arrived. Ah gien 'im yer names an' a'.'

'You what ! You gave him our names ! That was a cool thing to do. What would we want to go to a thing like that for ?'

'Ach away, Serah, Ah widda thocht an intelligent wumman like you widda seen the advantages right away. Ye never know —if Peter could only meet-in-wi' some o' the Big Bugs o' the BBC he could get a chance o' playin' on the wireless, like. See ?'

'Yes, but——'

'An' that chap M'Crepe, the meenister. Ah'm sure Maisie wid like fine if he got takin' yin o' thur broadcast services some Sunday night !'

'But I've just told you——'

'An' jist think hoo prood Wullie wid be tae meet the Lord Provost.'

At that point Sarah committed the tactical error of asking the price of the tickets.

'Five shillin's each!' he almost sprang upon her in his eagerness and triumph. 'But conseederin' hoo much ye'll get oota it, they're cheap at the price.'

'Five shillings each? Four of them—that's a pound!' she was showing less interest now.

But the crafty one knew how to handle her. 'Ay—it seems a lot when ye say it like that, but Ah'm sure thon wumman M'Cotton wid gie five pound if *she* could get invited.'

That was a shrewd one, she realised ; then, to disguise her capitulation, she said, 'What if Willie won't go?'

'You wait till ye get 'im in the richt mood, Serah. Gie 'im ham an' twa eggs fur 'is tea the night.'

'And where,' she asked, 'would I get the ham and eggs to do it with?'

'Ach, Ah wis jist speakin' efter a manner o' speakin'. Ye'll take them then?'

'I don't know. A pound's an awful lot of money. I like to put past so-much every week in the Savings Bank, you know.'

'But, Serah, think on the investment this wid be! If Peter got playin' on the wireless he'd maybe get as much as a pound a night.'

'Oh, I don't think Peter's as good as all that—a whole pound for a night's playing!'

'Well, but even if he got yin o' theym whit-ye-ma-ca'-its —an audition?'

'Well,' she hesitated.

'An' Ah'm sure Maisie wid take a second notion tae the meenister chap, if she heard 'im on the wireless.'

'Oh, be quiet and let me think!'

'Away—ye don't need tae think, Serah. Ah'm sure you wid like fine tae dae somethin' tae brag aboot tae thon M'Cotton wife. Jist think hoo chawed she'd be if she heard youse were goin' tae a thing like this an' she wisnae.'

' I suppose she would,' she agreed slowly. Slowly also she moved across the kitchen to where her purse lay.

Mattha followed her ; snatched the pound note. ' Ye'll no' regret it, Serah,' he assured her. Pocketing the money he said, ' Ah'll jist pit the tickets up on the mantelpiece here, see. Ah'm feart the envelope's a bit clarty, but Ah wis 'ilin' the man's nock, ye see. Ah'll away, well.'

' As quick as that ? What's your hurry ? I'm just coming out my messages.'

He was halfway out of the house before she had finished. Yelling ' Tell Willie Ah wis askin' fur'm,' he slammed the door and was gone. All that remained now was to talk Willie into accompanying her to the BBC ceremony ; Peter and Maisie, she knew, would co-operate out of natural curiosity.

2

Schooling herself to be patient with her husband's irritating mannerisms which seemed particularly maddening that evening, Sarah said nothing of Mattha's visit, hoping for an improvement in his temper before bedtime. When a sock she was darning fell into his basin of soapy water, however, her restraint gave way.

' Oh, Willie,' she burst out, ' I wish you'd give up this habit of steeping your feet every Friday night. That basin just clutters up the whole fireside.'

' Ach, lea'e me alane ! Ah thocht when Ah got halibut fur ma tea the night ye must be feelin' saft tae me, but noo ye're naggin' as hard as ever.'

' Well, you'd feel like nagging too if you were me.' Then to show how impartial was her rod of correction, she turned on Maisie and said, ' Here, could you not shift that pile of exercise books over a bit. I can't even get a corner of the table.'

Maisie was too wrapped up in her work to worry much about the quality of her mother's tones. ' Okay,' she said blithely. 'Would you listen to this. History exercise from a girl of twelve : *Mary Queen of Scots was never known to smile. This was because she had rotting teeth.* I ask you ! '

'Oh, poor soul,' said Sarah, keeping a grip on her temper, 'she'll be trying to be polite. She likely thinks that *rotting* sounds better than *rotten.*'

'But that's not the point, Mother. Here's me been dinning into my class the history of the reign of Mary, week in and week out. And when they're asked to write an essay on the subject, this moron goes and concocts this rubbish.'

'My, isn't it wonderful the names they think up nowadays ! ' observed Sarah, deciding not to say ' BBC ' just yet, ' I've never heard of " Moron " before. D'you think it's made up from " Marion " ? '

With mock patience Maisie explained that a moron was a half-wit, and with mock humility Sarah retorted that she supposed she was the half-wit for saying it.

'Oh dear,' she sighed, dismissing the subject from her mind instantaneously, ' these socks of Peter's—I wonder if he's got nails sticking up inside his shoes ? I'll need to darn them with string, I think. Look at the holes—Maisie, look at them,' she pleaded.

But Maisie was too occupied with her own problems. ' Oh, this is fantastic ! ' she cried. ' *Mary Queen of Scots was very beautiful that is why Queen Elizabeth was jealous of her. There is a whole lot of beds all over England where Queen Elizabeth slept.* My sainted aunt ! '

'It should be *There are a whole lot of beds*, shouldn't it ! ' said Sarah conversationally.

'Oh, forget it ! '

For a moment or two there was silence except for the tinkle of music which came from the sitting-room where Peter, with the Youth Club concert in mind, was closeted with his fiddle. Suddenly it seemed to pierce Willie's consciousness. Without even a grunt of warning he shouted, ' Heh, fur the luva mike, Serah, can ye no' stop that cat's concert ben the hoose ? '

'Now, Willie,' Sarah tried to keep calm, for she had been

on the point of raising the matter of the BBC, ' that's not the way to speak about your own son. He's doing his best. And if he's to be playing at the concert he's got to practise.'

' Help ma boab, when Ah think o' the row you kicked up ower the heid o' Mr McPlaid's bagpipes—an' everybody kens a fiddle's mair penetratin' ! '

At that moment the door-bell ringing, Willie took advantage of the circumstance to say, ' There ye are, whit did Ah tell ye ! That's the folk f'ae three closes away.'

' Don't be silly. Maisie, you go to the door, and don't bring anybody in here.'

' Whit wey no' ? ' asked Willie innocently as Maisie swept out impatiently.

' What ! And you with your dirty big feet in that basin.'

' They're no' durty ! ' He fetched one dripping foot out of its screen of soapsuds and held it up for her to see. ' Look—it's cleaner nur yours, Ah'll bet ! '

But Sarah was not heeding. All her listening faculties were strained towards what was happening on her doorstep.

' Good gracious ! ' she exclaimed, ' it's that woman M'Cotton! Fancy her having the nerve to come here after what happened the last time ! '

' Ach—camel-face ! ' remarked Willie who had a short memory.

' Get you out of that basin this minute ! '

' Ah'm no' *in* the basin, but !—jist ma feet ! '

Clutching at the strings of her overall, she wrenched it off ; then catching sight of certain intimate garments strung across the ceiling, she wrenched them from the pole and poked them behind the cushions on the bed-settee. ' How is it that that woman always knows when to come when she's least wanted ? Come on, Willie, hurry up ! She's caught you before like this.'

' Ah'm no' stoppin' steepin' ma feet fur a' the M'Cottons in the world ! ' he declared. ' Ah've steeped ma feet every Friday night since Ah came oot the airmy. An' forbye, ye're jist new-done tellin' Maisie no' tae bring onybody in here ! '

' But you know what that woman is—she'll force her way in anywhere ! '

As if in support of her statement the door opened and Maisie started to make some sort of apologetic statement which was shouted down by the woman behind her.

' Good evening, Mrs McFlehnnel,' she said, advancing into the kitchen in spite of the wall of hostility barring her way, ' Maisie wanted me to go into the lounge—ehm, you call it parlour of course, don't you ?—but Eh just said Eh was practically a member of the femily, so Eh insisted on coming in here. Eh haven't got tehm for ceremony. Eh just rushed up to tell you the latest excitement.'

Sarah told herself to keep calm as she said, ' Oh, the fire's on in the sitting-room. Peter's practising there so we'll just go.'

' That's what I told her, Mother,' said Maisie, ' but she insisted on coming in here.' And having thus washed her hands of the whole affair she sat down at the table once again and became immersed in her exercise corrections.

' It's not wirth meh while ! ' said Mrs M'Cotton, sitting down and thus moving out of the line of Sarah's ample screen. ' Oh, you're there, Mr McFlehnnel. Eh didn't notice you.'

' Hoo' ye,' said Willie more from annoyance than embarrassment.

' Perhaps we might be as well to go into the—um— sitting-room after all. Eh don't want to make you feel uncomfortable.'

' Ye're no' makin' me feel uncomfortable, missus,' said Willie calmly. ' Sit doon again. Ah suppose yer ain man washes 'is feet noo an' again ? '

' He does nothing of the kind. Eh mean—Mr M'Cotton has a beth every night ! '

' Aw but Ah'm no' as durty as a' that,' retorted Willie, ' he must surely be an awfu man fur sweetin'.'

' Willie, don't be vulgar,' said Sarah, sitting down in the presence of the inevitable.

' Good gracious ! ' exclaimed the visitor with her head on

one side listening with exaggeration, ' isn't thet next-door wireless loud ! Thet's the wirst of living in a tenement ! '

' That's no' a wireless set—that's oor Peter scrapin' a hair oota the tail o' a deid horse across the inside o' a deid cat ! ' said Willie, hoping he had got the phrase right.

' Eh don't know what you're talking about. All Eh know is —it's very like a piece we heard on the wireless the other night. You wouldn't be listening to it, of course. It was on the Third Programme.'

Ignoring the sneer for the simple reason that she did not quite know what the Third Programme signified, Sarah said that Peter was practising for a concert.

' Is that so ? Well, Eh reely haven't tehm to hear all the details. Eh just dropped up to tell you that an invitation has came for Mr M'Cotton and Eh to go to Margaret McVelvet's wedding ! '

From the region of the table came a fervent, ' Well, of all the heart-breaks—— '

Unaware of the source of Maisie's grief, Mrs M'Cotton said, ' Dear me, Maisie, you don't need to take it like that, surely. Eh knew you'd be jealous, of course, but Eh didn't expect you to make it quate so plain.'

' What the antimacassar are you talking about ? ' asked Maisie in astonishment.

' Eh'm talking about the way you're so disappointed at not being invited to Margaret McVelvet's wedding ! '

' Me ? Disappointed ? ' gulped the girl, ' it's the first I've heard of the affair. What I'm all het-up about is this essay. Listen to this : *Mary Queen of Scots was a French woman and she was married a lot of times. Men fought jewels over her, and their blood can still be seen in Edinburgh Castle.* Did you ever hear such a collection of inaccuracies ? '

' Eh never approved of Mary Queen of Scots,' declared Mrs M'Cotton, elongating her neck still farther, ' but as Eh was saying—— '

Unwilling to be reminded of what her friend had been saying Sarah rushed into speech :

'Maisie's had a terrible time with her class teaching them history !'

With the same end in view her husband rushed after her :

'Ach, there must be somethin' wrang wi' the wey ye're teachin' them, Maisie. Ah can mind when Ah wis at school——'

'As Eh was saying——' repeated Mrs M'Cotton a degree or two louder.

'Yes, Dad,' said Maisie, also in the conspiracy, 'I bet you can remember the dates of all the principal battles in British history, but what's the good of just knowing dates ? Can you remember the reasons for the battles being fought ?'

Once again the visitor reminded them : 'As Eh was saying the now——'

'Ach, you an' yer new-fangled notions !' said Willie, but he addressed his daughter and not the indignant lady opposite him.

'I'd rather have a pupil give me a date that was fifty years out, so long as he or she knew——'

Taking her vocal cords in both tonsils, as it were, Mrs M'Cotton shouted, 'The wedding ! The wedding's to be on the sixth of December—in the Cathedral, of course.'

Sarah was the only one who could bring herself to comment on the information. All she could say was, 'That'll be nice.'

'Eh thought Eh'd let you know in plenty of tehm so's you could make arrangements to go and see the guests going in, Mrs McFlehnnel. You've got so few pleasures !'

Sarah's indignation boiled up within her and bubbled over in rashness.

'Oh, I wouldn't be too sure of that, Mrs M'Cotton. As a matter of fact, for one thing, we've all been invited to the opening of the new BBC club.'

'Whit the——' began Willie, but Sarah's rashness was not yet exhausted.

'It was a great surprise, but we're all looking forward to it.'

'Ye gods and little fishes !' blurted out Maisie, 'what's this in aid of ?'

Fortunately Mrs M'Cotton was too eager to avoid hearing

any more unhistorical quotations to heed Maisie, so the surprise was overlooked as she exclaimed :

' Dear me, Mrs McFlehnnel, how did youse manage to get invited to a thing like that ?   Eh'm sure you'll all be like fish out of water.'

Willie tried again : ' But here, Serah——'

' You shouldn't judge everybody by yourself, Mrs M'Cotton. Just because *you* might feel like a fish out of water ! '

Tit-for-tat, Mrs M'Cotton replied that she didn't know that she'd care to be mixed up with people of that sort.

' What sort ? ' asked Sarah, turning a blind eye to her husband's gesticulations.

' Oh, Bohemians.   You know—velvet trousers and sandals. But Eh still don't understand how *youse* got invited.'

' It was through a friend of Mr McFlannel's,' stated Sarah categorically.

But Mrs M'Cotton had had enough, and shouting down Willie's hiccoughing protests she said with emphasis, ' Margaret's being married in oyster satin, so much nicer than——'

Inspired by her own imagination and goaded by her husband's eagerness to express himself, Sarah interrupted her friend with :

' All the big people in the BBC are to be there, of course. What's his name—Howard Lockhart——'

' Eh never heard of him !   As Eh was saying——'

Maisie who had apparently abandoned the fiction of the past for the fiction of the present, nipped in with :

' Oh, Mrs M'Cotton, don't say you've never heard of Howard Lockhart !   He's the biggest man on the BBC staff ! '

' She's having no less than six bridesmaids, Mrs McFlehnnel,' insisted Mrs M'Cotton in deplorable lack of interest.

' The Lord Provost is to be there too ! ' said Sarah.

' Mrs McVelvet said nothing to Mr M'Cotton and Eh about that !   How do you know ? '

' Oh, I'm not talking about the wedding,' said Sarah, and to her amazement her husband had lapsed into silence, ' I'm telling you about this BBC affair we're going to ! '

Mrs M'Cotton got to her feet.   ' Reely, Mrs McFlehnnel, Eh

think you're being very selfish. Here's me gone to all the trouble of coming to tell you all the details about this fashionable wedding ; but there, Eh might of knew you wouldn't appreciate a thing that's quate outside your kind of life. Eh'll have to be going.'

'But I haven't told you the rest about this BBC club,' said Sarah, also getting to her feet. 'Don't say you're jealous because we've been invited and you haven't !'

'Of course Eh'm not jealous ! But Eh still don't understand how a common wirking man like Mr McFlehnnel should be in touch with the BBC, and Mr M'Cotton, who's mixing with the highest in the land every day through his business, hasn't even heard about this club. Eh hope you all know how to conduct yourselves when you get there.'

'I'll see you to the door,' said Sarah somewhat unnecessarily, for she was already in the lobby with the visitor.

Willie, left alone with his daughter, demanded :

'Whit the bleezes is yer mother up tae noo ? Whit's a' this aboot ?'

'Search me, Dad. But we had to stand by her against the M'Cotton Queen !'

'Jeengs !' he exclaimed in admiration, 'whitna imagination she's got ! A' that blether aboot the BBC. Ah wid nevera gien 'er credit fur haein' it in 'er ! Boy, but that wumman M'Cotton disnae hauf gie me the boak. An' in case yer eddication hasnae learnt ye whit the boak is, it's scunner in plain English !'

'I know, Dad, only scunner isn't English any more than boak. But I get the drift of your remarks.' With a sigh she turned towards the table again, and bowed her head over the exercise books. 'What have we here ? *Mary Queen of Scots was beheaded because there was not room on the throne for two queens at one time.*'

Sarah came back into their midst saying that that woman M'Cotton would be the death of her yet.

'Never mind, lass,' said Willie in continued admiration, 'ye got the better o' 'er the night. A' the same it wis a peety ye had tae tell lees.'

'I didn't tell any lies. We really have got invitations!'

'Suffering saints!' Maisie abandoned her homework once again, 'why did you not tell us before now?'

'Because I was waiting to get your father in a good mood.'

'Ah!' spluttered Willie, 'so that's whit the halibut wis fur!'

'B-but—' Maisie struggled with her memories of the *contretemps*, 'who was Dad's friend that wangled the business?'

'Ay, tell me that!'

'Now don't start bullying me, Willie!' complained the woman. 'I only did it for the best. Did you hear her blowing about them getting an invitation to Margaret McVelvet's wedding? Fancy them being invited and us not!'

Had it not been for the saponaceous quality of his foothold Willie would have got to his feet and shaken his wife. As it was, he thundered, 'Never mind the McVelvet waddin'! Whit's this aboot invitations tae the BBC? Come on, oot wi't!'

'Well, it was this forenoon—your brother Mattha was here.' Since blame was afoot she might as well blame Willie for having a brother.

'But Uncle Matt's not a friend, Mother—he's a relation!'

'I know,' said Sarah patiently, 'but if I'd said Mattha to her she'd 've put her nose in the air.'

'You could hardly have blamed her. Go on, Mother.'

'Well, he said he'd got those tickets—four of them—through a man he'd been mending a clock for that works in the BBC.'

Maisie asked, 'Which of them works in the BBC? The man or the clock?'

'Oh, don't interrupt me! I didn't want to have anything to do with the affair, but, well—Mattha went on and on about how pleased the Lord Provost would be to see you, Willie, and——'

That shook Willie. 'Whit? Me? Ah'm sure Ah widnae ken whit tae say tae a Lord Provost unless Ah wis tae ask 'im whit wey oor ashpits isnae emp'ied regular.'

Maisie-the-teacher could not refrain from pointing out that control of salvage collection did not lie within the probable scope of the Lord Provost's duties.

'He's heid o' the Corporation, is 'e no'? A' he's got tae dae is tae whustle an' it rains blue snaw!'

'What other inducement did Uncle Matt offer?' continued Maisie.

'Well, he spoke about how nice it would be if Mr M'Crepe got the chance of preaching at a broadcast service some Sunday night.' Before she had finished speaking she realised she had committed a tactical error. Maisie's face grew red and thunderous but the opening of the kitchen door prevented her from giving voice to her embarrassed indignation.

'Oh, and—' glad of the excuse, Sarah beamed on Peter as he came in, 'he said you might get an audition or something, Peter.'

'Eh?' gulped the lad.

Maisie took the matter in hand. 'Look, Peter, sit down or hold on to something while I break the news to you in words of one syllable. It appears that, thanks in some mysterious way to Uncle Matt of all people, we've been invited to some sort of " do " in connection with the opening of the BBC club.'

'What? Us?' Peter's astonishment was complete.

'Ay—an' Ah'm expected tae chum up wi' the Lord Provost an' talk tae'm aboot ashpits,' said Willie.

'When is the exact date of the affair, Mother?' asked Maisie.

'Tomorrow night. I thought it would be a fine chance for me to wear my black velvet dress that I haven't had on since the Silver Wedding.'

'Well, Ah'm no' goin'—that's flat!' observed Willie, drying his foot.

'Neither am I,' said Peter. 'I couldn't grow a beard in time, and I've used my corduroy breeks for digging the plot in.'

Sarah said, 'I don't know what you're talking about, Peter. And as for you, Willie, what's the use of having that dinner-jacket suit if you never wear it?'

'Does it say " Evening Dress " on the tickets?'

'I never looked,' Sarah confessed. 'Your Uncle Mattha put them up there on the mantelpiece, and I was in such a hurry to get out my messages that I never even opened the envelope.'

Peter got up, and while he was opening the envelope his father expressed himself with intensity on the utter improbability of his being present at the affair.

'But, Willie,' pleaded Sarah, 'just think how nice it would be if it meant that Peter would be playing on the wireless some day. Fancy, your son's playing coming through your own wireless set!'

'Ah can hardly staun it comin' through three walls!' was Willie's retort.

'Listen, Mother,' said Peter in some bewilderment, 'these invitations——'

But she ignored his interruption. 'Well, then, Willie, would you not come for the sake of . . .' but a sidelong glance at Maisie's threatening face decided her against continuing that line of argument.

Peter tried again, but with no more success, for his mother was declaring hysterically that they would have to go to the affair now—after her boasting to Mrs M'Cotton about it.

'Mother,' yelled Peter, 'how much did Uncle Matt rush you for these tickets?'

'Well, I *did* think it was a lot of money, but after all, if we're meeting all these important people——'

'How much, Mum?'

'Don't shout at me like that, Peter. I'm not asking you to pay me—all I'm asking is for you to come with me.'

He tried soft persuasion, 'How much did the wee twister get out of you?'

'He said the tickets were five shillings each.'

In disgust Maisie turned back to her exercise books, saying that, as far as she was concerned, she wouldn't pay five shillings —not even to see Howard Lockhart.

'Surely, though,' said Sarah in self-defence, 'for all that money there'll be a dinner or something.'

This put a pleasant thought into her husband's mind, for he went so far as to say that if he thought there would be ham and egg on the menu he would put on two dinner jackets for the occasion.

Peter flourished the tickets in front of them. 'Listen, everybody. Mother, you've been swindled ! Look, these aren't tickets—they're invitations ! '

Peering at the pieces of cardboard, Sarah exclaimed, ' But what's R.S.V.P. doing on them ? I thought that was only for wedding invitations.' Pressed for an explanation of this extraordinary statement, she said, ' I thought R.S.V.P. stood for Remember and Send Valuable Presents, although I've always thought it looked awful cheeky.'

' But Mum,' said Peter, ' don't you see—that's not the point.' He kept waving the tickets exasperatingly. ' You didn't need to pay anything for these—they're invitations.'

Imitatively, Maisie growled, ' Imagine that ! ' but the Mattha touch was ignored by the others.

' Well—I—never ! ' gasped Sarah. ' D'you know, I thought Mattha went away awful quick after I'd given him the pound note. Oh dear-dear ! I don't think I want to go now.'

Willie smiled in quiet triumph as he bent to put on his clean socks ; his belief in his immunity from the rigours of winter had been once again justified. As for Peter, he did his best to comfort his worried mother by pointing out that the function, according to the tickets, had been held a fortnight previously.

Uncomforted, Sarah sighed, ' Oh dear-dear ! A whole pound note down the stank, to say nothing of that halibut for your tea, Willie ! '

With a snort of derision, Maisie turned from the villainies of the present to her pupils' conceptions of the villainies of the past.

CHAPTER 12

ANOTHER SPRIG ON THE FAMILY TREE

I

POLLY was once again in need of help, this time because she was expecting her third baby ; and the two grandmothers were pressed into service. Mrs M'Cotton got in first and came away with the lesser of two evils, the quiet little Moira, so Ian fell to the lot of the McFlannels for the chastisement of their respective bodies and souls. The understanding was that the children would be kept in Glasgow for three weeks, but after a fortnight Ian's undisciplined behaviour so exhausted the family that they were glad to invent an excuse to accompany him home to Edinburgh. At first Willie had refused to become a member of the escort party, pleading that no self-respecting Glaswegian ever went to Edinburgh if he could help it, that the only good thing that ever came out of Edinburgh was the Glasgow train, that he was not greatly interested in his latest grandchild and could, without difficulty, restrain himself from looking upon it until such time as it was able to come and see him. These and other extravagant statements were dealt with so adequately by his wife that he was on the train with the rest of his family that Saturday afternoon.

As for Mrs M'Cotton, her early enthusiasm having worn thin, she, too, decided to take her charge home a week earlier, with the result that both contingents met. Willie, leaning out of a non-smoking compartment with his pipe belching, was the first to see the approach of his other grandchild and was for drawing back, but Moira had seen him and hailed him with such glee that he was compelled to open the door for the newcomers.

When everyone was seated, the two grandmothers inspected

each other's charges. Said Mrs M'Cotton, ' Hullo, Ian, you're looking very pinched. What have you been doing with yourself ? '

Before the boy had time to tell her, Sarah said, ' That's funny, I was just thinking the same about wee Moira ! Has she not been eating her usual ? '

' She's been eating very well indeed,' was the indignant retort. ' Oh, beh the way, she doesn't know anything yet about the b-a-b-y. Eh thought it better that her Daddy should break the news to her.'

Ian, who up till now had been taking imaginary aim at the passengers in an adjacent train, turned round suddenly, saying, ' Grannie M'Cotton, I've got a new wee baby brother ! ' and while the lady addressed was trying to shush him in the interests of his sister's innocence, he added, ' Granpa says its name is " Dear-kens ".'

The starting of the train covered some of the ensuing embarrassment. After a bit, Mrs M'Cotton said :

' Eh was just saying to Mr M'Cotton that Eh hoped there wouldn't be any nonsense this tehm about fency names for the baby. Polly has had her own way over Ian and Moira, but Eh reely think this tehm she should show some respect for Dick and call the baby after Mr M'Cotton.'

To which Maisie retorted teacherishly, ' I think it's ridiculous —this habit of calling children after relations.'

' Oh, of course, Maisie. Eh can quate understand your feelings in the matter. Eh'd hate to be called " Maisie "—especially after the kehnd of person your Ent Maisie was.'

Sarah flared up. ' Mrs M'Cotton, how dare you say things like that about my sister that's been in her grave for twenty years ! '

To save the situation Peter threw himself into the gap in the undiplomatic relations. ' I was suggesting to Maisie that seeing Polly's always been so mad on the pictures, she'll maybe call the kid after some film star. We thought about Bing and Sinatra, but my vote goes to Wallace Beery. I think Beery M'Cotton would sound wizard ! '

Mrs M'Cotton thought it sounded disgusting and said so.

'If Ah had ma way o't,' said Willie from the corridor, 'Ah'd cry the wean efter ma faither—Mattha wis his name.'

'Never!' retorted Mrs M'Cotton. 'It reminds me too much of your brother Mattha.'

Open hostilities might have broken out there and then had it not been for the fact that Sarah had never disguised her dislike of her brother-in-law. As it was, the journey was completed in increasing discomfort for those who were compelled to listen to the innuendo and jealous retorts that passed between the two grandmothers. As they left the train at Waverley Station, Mrs M'Cotton grasped Moira firmly by the hand and hurried off to get a taxi, a luxury which the more thrifty McFlannels were apt to describe as 'pure swank.' As she disappeared into the crowd, Moira's escort called back, 'Eh'm going to insist on Dick calling the baby "James"! If he doesn't, then Eh'll never speak to Polly again.'

Completely unconcerned about both her desires and her threats, the McFlannel party travelled by the more tortuous method of Corporation transport, finally arriving at the front gate of Polly's pretentious villa. Although she had seen it frequently before, Sarah could not refrain from exclaiming, 'My, what a lovely drive up to the house!'

To which Willie, in disgust, retorted, 'As lang as the drive leads away f'ae the hoose Ah'll no' grumble,' a statement that drew forth from Sarah a word of warning when they ultimately arrived on the doorstep:

'Now see here, Willie—before we ring the bell—is it any use asking you to try and behave yourself?'

'Behave masel'? Ah'm no' a wean! An' onywey Polly kens fine whit 'er faither's like. It's nae use tryin' tae create a guid impression noo.'

'It's not Polly I'm thinking about—it's Mrs M'Cotton. Try not to let her see you're frightened of Polly's big house.'

'Ah'm no' frightened. Ye shouldnae judge everybody by yersel'.'

Just as Peter was stretching out his hand towards the bell handle, Willie pleaded for a minute's grace.

'Here, if it's a lassie in a fancy apern that opens the door, dae Ah gie 'er ma hat an' coat ? '

'No,' said Peter, 'just your carpet slippers.'

'Eh ? Ah havenae got nae carpet slippers wi' me, but ! '

'So long as you don't shake hands with her you'll do, Dad,' said Maisie.

2

Fortunately for Willie's peace of mind it was Polly herself who opened the door, having heard the murmurings. When the initial greetings were over and Ian had been compared with his appearance a fortnight previously, Maisie shook her sister by the arm and demanded to know where the baby was. At that moment Mrs M'Cotton emerged from the lounge, saying, 'Eh've been here for heff an hour, Maisie, and Eh haven't seen him yet. It's well seen Dick isn't here or he wouldn't of allowed his mother to be treated like this.'

Polly said, 'But I explained to you already, Grannie, that the nurse believes in keeping very strictly to her schedule. And besides, you're all here a week earlier than you promised ! '

The guilty parties avoided each other's eyes and trooped into the lounge where they sat holding phatic communion, until Sarah could restrain herself no longer.

'Oh, Polly, have you and Dick made up your minds yet about what you're going to call the baby ? '

'Eh've just been telling her,' Mrs M'Cotton snapped, 'that it will be a positive insult to Dick's father and Eh if it's not going to be " James." Or even " Hamish " if they must have something fancy—that's the Gaelic for " James ".'

There was an instant clamour of disagreement, Maisie declaring her theories about the absurdity of sticking to tribal names, Peter advocating the impartiality of film-star nomenclature, Sarah pleading for compromise and Ian demanding to be allowed to play with his toy trumpet.

'Polly,' said Willie, ' you dae whit ye want tae dae, lass, an' never heed ony o' them. Ca' the wean Nebuchadnezzar if ye like.'

' Willie, don't be vulgar,' exclaimed Sarah. Just then all eyes were turned towards the door which had opened. The nurse, carrying the baby, came into the room. Polly, in her younger days, had been interested in amateur dramatic shows, so Maisie watched her sister somewhat cynically as she went forward and took the baby in her arms amid the tense silence. Mrs M'Cotton broke it by blurting out, ' Now, Polly——'

But Polly ignored the interruption, just as she ignored the clamant hands of her two elder children who wanted to see the baby's face. She walked across the room to where her father stood in obvious disgust with the petty wrangling.

' Here you are, Dad,' she said with unbelievable affection and simple sincerity, ' Dick and I have made up our minds he's to be called " William McFlannel M'Cotton " ! '

The emotional import of the gesture was too much for her mother who burst out, ' Oh, Polly, that's the nicest thing you've ever done in all your life ! '

Willie, for his part, was also touched, but speech did not come easily to him in his spiritual crises. He sniffed, twitched his nose and awkwardly pushed the baby back into his daughter's arms again, saying, ' Heh, take the wean ! Ah think Ah've got a cauld comin' on an' Ah don't want tae smit 'im.'

While the rest of the McFlannels clustered round to see the face of this new scion, Mrs M'Cotton made an indignant departure from the house, no-one, however, noticing her absence until much later. In any case they were uncomfortably aware that she would crop up again sooner or later, like Maisie's suitors.